Gemma Sommerset

"*Gemma Sommerset* is a charming, satisfying catharsis of a book, a story of love and loss and secrets. I love everything about this novel—its magical setting, where sky meets mountain, the vibrant prose and compelling characters, but most of all, Gemma, my new favorite heroine who encourages an unforgettable, powerful question: Who is it that we really want to become in our lives?"

—Kim Bradley, *Spillway*

"As we age, it seems the years flash by, and the same is true for Gemma Sommerset. With concise and compact writing, Jill McCroskey Coupe depicts a Virginia woman who's true to herself and to her daughters as she seeks what we all seek in life: fulfilment and a happy ending. A refreshing and satisfying read."

—Louella Bryant, *Sheltering Angel*

"In her third novel, Jill McCroskey Coupe has brought into even stronger focus the meaning of the circle of life. As she deftly takes us on Gemma Sommerset's passages from childhood to old age, we realize that this is not just Gemma's story but our own. The action is well-developed and compelling. This is a book you cannot put down!"

—Julie Fritz, *Twinings: Poems at Eighty*

"After finishing Jill McCroskey Coupe's tender and riveting new novel, I was still seeing the world through its radiant lens. Reading *Gemma Sommerset* is like falling into a beguiling dream from which you don't want to wake. Here is a heartfelt and redemptive novel of love and loss so exquisitely told that you want to stand up and cheer for Gemma and her family and for the author who writes with such intelligence, grace, and tenderness."

—John Dufresne, *My Darling Boy*

Gemma Sommerset

A Novel

Jill McCroskey Coupe

Rootstock Publishing

Montpelier, VT

Author's Note

I began writing *Gemma Sommerset* early in 2019 and took a hurried first draft to John Dufresne's novel-writing workshop in Taos, New Mexico, that summer. Throughout the pandemic, and after my move in 2021 from Maryland to Vermont, I kept on writing and revising. In 2023, I followed Einstein's advice to simplify. This meant starting all over again, with a different structure for the novel and a new first chapter, but I don't regret it for a minute.

By setting much of the novel in Lexington, Virginia, I was giving myself an excuse to visit the town where my mother's father, her brother, and my cousin had all graduated from Washington and Lee University. Finally, in the summer of 2022, I was able to spend a few days in Lexington. This was not long enough, and I knew it at the time, but I hope the city's friendly inhabitants will forgive any mistakes I've made. How friendly? One morning, as I sat sipping coffee on the front porch of my B&B, I was amazed at the number of dog walkers who smiled and waved to me.

During the pandemic, several librarians at the Rockbridge Regional Library System gave me very helpful details about Lexington via email. I thanked them then, and I'll thank them now.

Heartfelt thanks also to my son, Brad Coupe, and to my dear friend Joan Zelinka, both of whom read the manuscript in April of 2024 and gave me encouraging and perceptive feedback.

The letter Gemma's father, Carson, wrote home from Japan is, word-for-word, the letter my father, Joseph Stewart McCroskey, wrote to my mother, Hope Kimbrough McCroskey, in November of 1945. Neither of my parents ever lived in Virginia, however; Gemma and her family are entirely fictional.

"I am out with lanterns, looking for myself."
—Emily Dickinson,
letter to Elizabeth Holland, January 20, 1856

Part I
Love and Marriage

1

In the Blue Ridge Mountains, during her second summer at a girls' camp beside a lake in western North Carolina, Gemma Sommerset, from Lynchburg, Virginia, received a glimpse of who she really was, or could become. This was in 1957, when Gemma was fourteen.

A small group of campers had been given permission to go horseback riding early on a Sunday morning, with no counselor along to supervise. There were maybe ten of them, ten eager souls who'd saddled their horses in the dark. As the sun began to rise, the girls mounted up and, in single file, followed a dirt road leading from the horse barn to the trail that circled the lake.

By the time they'd reached the other side of it, the lake was nearly as pink as the sky. At a break in the trees, the girls stopped to gaze at the long row of shingled cabins where the less fortunate campers, and their counselors, were still asleep.

The riders then urged their horses on. For some reason, or no reason at all, whoever was in the lead turned onto a side trail.

This less-traveled trail headed up the mountain, then leveled out. Jumps appeared, with rails set higher than the girls were used to. A counselor, never identified, had neglected to remove the rails, which should have been lying harmlessly on the ground.

Perhaps that was the counselor who'd yelled at them when they returned to the barn that morning. The one who'd demanded, "What in the hell were you girls thinking?"

But of course, they hadn't been thinking at all, hadn't needed to, having been taught that if you simply give your horse its head, then the two of you will fly over the jump. And the next one. And the next.

The horses were going too fast that glorious morning. Soaring into the air at breakneck speed, then noisily galloping on to the next jump.

The girls hung on for dear life, grabbing hold of the manes, for which they would have been chastised in the ring. Experienced riders, they knew not to panic, understood that trusting their horses was the best way to stay safe.

For Gemma, each jump was simultaneously terrifying and exhilarating. Never had she felt so alive, so free. Pounding hoofbeats, then an eerie silence as she and her horse left the ground.

After flying over the last jump, she managed to slow her excited steed down. And then to descend, with the others, to the trail beside the lake, unaware, as yet, that they had awakened the entire camp.

Earlier that morning, an unexceptional teenager had saddled a horse before dawn. A courageous, capable young woman trotted back to the stables.

The person she most wanted to tell was Nat, her younger brother. Gnat, she'd secretly nicknamed him.

Several times, during the afternoon Quiet Hour, she tried to describe, in a letter to Nat, the thrilling, early-morning horseback ride. How she'd so easily soared over jumps higher than any she'd ever before encountered. And her feeling, afterwards, that she'd taken a dramatic step into the rest of her life, had glimpsed the brave and capable person she would turn out to be.

But while she was trying to find exactly the right words, it would begin to rain, as it often did at that time of day in the mountains. There was screening along the top third of the cabin's walls, over which canvas flaps could be lowered during a thunderstorm. But the afternoon rains were usually gentle, causing eyes to close, tensions to relax, worries to float away.

Lulled by the fresh smell of the rain, its soft drum-beats on the cabin's roof, Gemma would drift off. Awakening to clear skies, she would vow to try again.

And she did try, several times, to put her thoughts about that early-morning ride into words. It was her first failure as a writer.

2

On the last morning of camp, all her cabinmates, and even her counselor, had been picked up before noon. Hungry, Gemma walked down to the dining hall to see if lunch was being served.

Only one table was occupied. She sat down and stated the obvious: yes, she was still there. Her parents were coming all the way from the coast of South Carolina, so no, she wasn't the least bit worried about them.

Back in the empty cabin, Gemma lay down on a bare mattress. Instead of dozing off when the rains came, she entered a state of near panic, worried that something terrible had happened to her family.

For sentimental reasons, her parents spent a week at Myrtle Beach every summer. Myrtle Beach was where they'd met.

In August of 1940, Maryl Owings had been sitting alone on a bench on the Second Avenue Pier, when Carson Sommerset walked past with several of his friends.

He quickly turned around and went back.

"You look so sad," he said to Maryl.

When she didn't respond, he sat down beside her. And eventually, maybe because he hadn't said another word, she told him she'd once shared that very same bench with her father, who'd recently died, and even though she knew it wouldn't bring him back, she'd had a desperate need to sit there again.

And that was how a redhead from Columbus, Ohio, and a dark-haired young man from Lynchburg, Virginia, had fallen in love. Maryl had come to Myrtle Beach alone, by train. Carson had driven down with some friends from college, who, sooner than they'd planned, and with Maryl along for the ride, were on their way back to Virginia.

After Pearl Harbor, Carson enlisted in the Army. He then drove to Columbus and proposed to Maryl. It was in Columbus, two years later, with her father about to leave for Europe, that Gemma was born.

Wide awake in the otherwise empty cabin, Gemma was surprised when the camp director, wearing a wide-brimmed rain hat, came up the steps, knocked on the door, and asked if she could come in.

"Your parents will be here soon," she said, letting the

screen door bang shut behind her. "Your brother's been sick, but he's better now. Nothing to worry about."

"Nat?"

"No need to worry, he's fine."

Again, Gemma nodded.

"Would you like company while you wait?"

Gemma shook her head.

"You were one of those horseback riders, weren't you?"

"What horseback riders?"

"Someone might've been killed that morning, you know, or permanently injured. The camp could've been sued from here to kingdom come."

"I'll be fine by myself," Gemma said.

With a shrug of one shoulder, the director turned to leave. "Just so's you know, the dining hall won't be open tonight."

Again, the screen door slammed.

After some time, another knock on the door. Gemma sat up, then burst into tears.

"Everything's fine," her father said, closing the door softly behind him. "I told her to tell you not to worry, the woman I spoke to."

"I wasn't worried."

"That's good." He patted the top of her head, something he hadn't done since she was a child. "We missed you at the beach. Did you have a good summer?"

"Best one yet. How's Nat?"

"Much better. It was food poisoning, from the crabs he had for dinner last night, but we found a doctor this morning who gave him a shot. He's over the worst of it."

They carried her trunk up to where the car was parked. Nat was asleep in the back. Gemma lifted his bare feet, climbed in under them, and set the stinky feet on her lap.

Without opening his eyes, Nat gave her a small wave.

"Don't wake your brother up," Maryl said from the front seat. "He needs to rest."

Nat put a finger to his lips.

"We thought we'd find a motel for tonight," Carson said.

"Then tomorrow," Maryl said, "we'll take the Blue Ridge Parkway home."

Gemma tickled a bare foot, and Nat gave her a kick. How their mother *loved* the long, slow, seemingly neverending but oh-so-beautiful drive along the Blue Ridge Parkway!

"How was your summer?" Maryl said.

"Anything exciting happen?" Carson said.

"Exciting?" Gemma pretended to think this over.

She then told them about the canoe trip down a mountain stream so swollen by heavy rains that the rapids proved to be far more risky than the counselors had anticipated. The turbulent water slammed one of the canoes into a boulder, bending the aluminum craft into a perfect V, its bow and stern pointing skyward. The two paddlers were tossed into the roiling water.

After fishing them out, the counselors ended the excursion then and there. All canoes, including the damaged one, were dragged to dry ground. The group then followed a faint path down the mountain, to a road, a Good Samaritan in a pickup truck, and a happy ending.

"Were you scared?" her mother said.

"Seeing the canoe bent in half was scary. I had no idea that could happen. The girls got soaking wet, of course. Plus a few bruises. But no one was seriously hurt, even the two who'd been rescued." Another potential lawsuit the camp director had managed to avoid.

"Those girls were very lucky," her father said. "You should write that down when we get home. You have a real knack for storytelling."

"Not to mention melodrama," her mother added.

Nat's eyes opened. His lips silently formed the word: *mel-o-dra-ma.*

Gemma never told Nat, or anyone else, about her early-morning horseback ride. Or the feeling that she'd become a different person, with a new life ahead of her. Back in Lynchburg, in the same old house, she was still the same old Gemma, facing the same old parental expectations. Study hard, make good grades. With good grades, she could get into a good college. Once there, if she was lucky, the right sort of young man would ask her to marry him.

Because Maryl hadn't been so lucky, she'd gone on to graduate school. Then, with a master's degree in statistics, she'd taken a train to Myrtle Beach. The probability of an Ohio woman marrying a Virginia man she'd met on an ocean pier in South Carolina must have seemed to her so small as to have made the union seem divinely ordained.

3

By the time Gemma got her driver's license at sixteen, her mother was already thinking about college, preferably a coed school within driving distance from Lynchburg. Fontana, Gemma's best friend since kindergarten, was applying to schools out of state.

"What about Duke?" Gemma said to her mother. "Or Emory? Fontana and I could room together."

"Dr. Rollins can afford those schools. Your father can't."

"What if I got a scholarship?"

"We won't stop you from trying," her mother said. "But the likelihood of you and Fontana ending up at the same school is very small."

"Statistically speaking, you mean?" Gemma said. 'Statistically speaking' was one of her mother's favorite expressions.

"Approaching zero," Maryl said.

In kindergarten, the teacher had often asked the class to line up in alphabetical order, sometimes according to first names, at other times last names. Either way, Gemma Sommerset (carrot top) and Fontana Rollins (raven head) had ended up standing next to each other.

To Gemma's father, the girls were *The Red and the Black*. A novel he highly recommended, once they were old enough to appreciate it.

Having been accepted at both the University of Richmond and the College of William and Mary, Gemma chose Richmond, even though it didn't offer in-state tuition. Richmond was a big city—bigger than Lynchburg, anyway—with better job prospects once she'd graduated.

"If that's where you really want to go," her father said, "then we'll manage somehow."

"I've heard that wealthy New England families send their sons to Richmond," her mother said.

Halfway through her freshman year, Gemma began dating another freshman, Howard, who was from Houston, Texas. Howard said he loved her. Then he dumped her.

She decided to major in French. Went out with one of Howard's friends for a while. Spent a lot of time in the library. As did a stocky, sandy-haired young man.

One night, when he was seated across the table from

her, she looked up and realized it had begun to snow.

"Oh!" she said.

"Something wrong?" he said without looking up.

"It's snowing."

He glanced out the window. When he turned back, she noticed his eyes. Gray or blue? Impossible to tell, as the color kept changing.

"Would you like a ride home?" he said.

She'd seen snow before, and didn't mind walking back to her dorm. "That would be great."

"Let me just finish this chapter," he said.

On the way to his ancient Volkswagen, Tim McKenna told her he was putting himself through college with a part-time job as a bookkeeper. When he wasn't working, he was studying, and vice versa. He'd played football in high school, in Buena Vista, but didn't have time for college athletics.

"I'm from Lynchburg," she said.

"All right," he said softly, giving her a friendly punch in the arm.

Several times a week, they would meet up, at that same table. When the library closed, Tim would fold his six-foot frame into his small car and drive her back to her dorm. As a junior, Tim lived off campus, sharing an apartment with another student, a "drunken slob," which was why Tim didn't try to study there.

One night, as they were leaving the library, Tim offered her a Wint-O-Green Lifesaver and then popped one into his own mouth. When they arrived at her dorm, he turned off the engine and said, "Gemma from Lynchburg, is it OK if I kiss you?"

It seemed a silly question, so she didn't bother answering. They both tasted of mint.

Each night, while parked outside her dorm, they went a little bit farther. She let him touch her where no one ever had before. The windows steamed up.

On a Sunday afternoon in April, while exploring a wooded area at the edge of campus, they discovered a small dell surrounded by tall trees. A very private place.

The following Sunday, Tim spread a blanket on the carpet of dead leaves. They couldn't get carried away though, he warned. That would ruin everything.

"Like in that French movie you took me to see," he said.

"*The Umbrellas of Cherbourg.*"

"Yeah." He sat down on the blanket, took her hand, and pulled her down beside him. "I finally got used to all the singing, and the subtitles, but the story was a real drag."

"Because the mother insisted the daughter should get married. That's what ruined things."

Tim made a sound in his throat.

Gemma already knew about the plans he didn't want ruined. He would soon go off to graduate school, in Florida, for a master's degree in accounting. Florida, because his older sister lived in Tallahassee and he'd have free room and board. A quiet place to sleep. No longer would he have a roommate coming in roaring drunk nearly every night.

Gemma had plans of her own. A French professor had suggested a graduate program in Paris and even promised to write a letter of reference for her.

That Sunday afternoon, they lay side by side, staring up into swaying branches sprouting new green leaves. "This is so much better than the Volkswagen," Gemma said. "I love trees."

Tim rolled onto his side, touched her cheek. "I'm almost afraid to kiss you."

"Oh, go ahead."

She imagined they were in a French painting, by Renoir or Degas. Two lovers on a blanket in the woods.

Except that in France, the lovers would be naked. Gemma and Tim kept their clothes on. Buttons buttoned; zippers zipped.

4

In 1968, when Nat was in his final semester at Georgetown, he called Gemma, in Lynchburg, and asked if she'd go hiking with him, on his twenty-first birthday, in the Shenandoah National Park.

"Just the two of us," he said. "Anywhere you want to go."

"The Limberlost," she said.

"I knew you'd say that."

Nat took a bus from DC, arriving in Lynchburg on a Friday night. Early the next morning, in their father's Datsun, they headed north, with Nat driving.

"When were you going to tell me you're engaged?" he said.

Gemma glanced at the ring Tim had given her. "I'm not sure I am. It was Tim's grandmother's ring. He handed it to me on New Year's Eve and asked if it fit."

"So you tried it on, and then you kept it."

"What else was I supposed to do?"

Tim had returned from Florida with a graduate degree in accounting, but Gemma never made it to

Paris. Carson had deemed the program's tuition, plus room and board, to be "too rich for his blood." When Gemma countered that she could get a part-time job in Paris, find a room to rent, Maryl, despite having a master's degree of her own, nixed that idea. Instead of studying in the City of Love, she taught high school French in Richmond for a year. Then, because Tim was back in Buena Vista and not happy about having to drive all the way to Richmond to see her, she found a similar teaching job, three days a week, in Lynchburg. Living at home instead of renting an apartment almost made up for the reduction in pay.

"What're you going to do after you graduate?" she asked her brother.

"Find a way to avoid the draft." Nat thought the war in Vietnam had been wrong from the very beginning. "That's what I wanted to talk to you about."

"We could go to Paris, both of us."

"Mais oui," he said.

Once they were on the Skyline Drive, gliding along with the windows open, their spirits lifted. The sky was a brilliant blue, the mountain air cool and fragrant.

"This is heaven," Nat said. "DC's OK, but nothing beats these mountains."

"And here's our place of worship." Gemma pointed to a sign for the Limberlost Trail.

From the parking lot, a path led into a forest of old-growth hemlocks whose lush needles split the sunlight into pale green rays. Long before the creation of the Shenandoah National Park, a married couple had bought this tract of land so as to preserve the old-growth hemlocks and prevent them from ever being cut down and hauled away by loggers.

Decades later, the ancient trees seemed to have gained mystical powers. Honoring the eerie silence, visitors to this green cathedral knew to tread quietly, whispering to each other if they spoke at all.

Nat took a deep breath. "I'm thinking about going to Canada," he whispered.

"Good for you," Gemma whispered back.

They walked on in silence. When she pointed to the sign for the White Oak Canyon Trail and raised her eyebrows, Nat nodded. They turned off, headed downhill.

"Do you think I should leave the country?" he said. "Even with our dear father serving on the Lynchburg draft board?"

"Especially so. I don't know why he ever thought that was a good idea." Although she did. Carson had told her he hoped his could be a voice of reason.

Nat had already spent time in a foreign country. A month in Scotland one summer, as part of an exchange program between Glasgow, Virginia, and Glasgow, Scotland. And then, in college, a junior semester in Zurich. Gemma had never been anywhere.

"Dad will be furious if I run off to Canada," Nat said.

"It's your life," she said. "Maybe I'll come with you. Fontana's in Vancouver, living with a professor she had at Emory. Last I heard, anyway."

"What about Tim?"

"He can come, too, if he wants. Canadians must need accountants."

"You really think he would?"

She didn't. Having spent nearly two years in Tallahassee, Tim was back in Buena Vista, working with an elderly accountant whose clients Tim hoped to inherit.

"The thing is," she said, "if your name comes up, Dad won't play favorites. He's too honorable for that."

"But I'll embarrass him if I go to Canada. His own son a draft-dodger. When there are so many, many brave soldiers in our family tree. All the way back to the Civil War."

"He was in the Army long enough so that you shouldn't have to be. Our family qualifies for a blanket exemption from ever having to fight in another war."

"Especially this one. It's as misguided as fighting to preserve slavery was." Nat sat down on a boulder. "If I go to Canada, then I can't ever come home again."

"I'll visit you. Don't worry. I bet Mom and Dad will, too."

"I thought you were coming with me."

"I don't know what to do." She sat down beside him. "I'm *so* mixed up."

"Oh, Gemma." Nat touched her arm. "What's going on?"

It was what was not going on that bothered her. Nearly every Saturday night, Tim drove to Lynchburg in his VW. After parking on a dark road, he would spend hours kissing and touching her, wanting her to touch him.

Let's get in back, she'd said one night.

He was too tall, he'd said. There wasn't enough room.

We could find a spot in the woods, she'd pleaded. Like we did in Richmond.

No, he'd said. We have to wait.

But sex was not something she could discuss with her little brother. "Tim doesn't read," she said.

"He can't read? But he has a master's degree."

"He read textbooks, because he had to. He doesn't read for pleasure, though. Not ever."

"What does he do in his spare time?" Nat said.

"Watches golf on TV," she said.

"Well, so does Dad."

"But Dad reads. He's always reading."

"Yeah. Even while he's watching TV."

Nat pulled Gemma to her feet, and they continued on down the trail. He said he'd heard Toronto was the best entry point. You could get to Ontario by crossing the Peace Bridge in Buffalo, and then Toronto was just a few miles away.

"But I should probably figure out where the job opportunities are. I'll need to eat."

"Quebec," Gemma said. "I could teach French there."

"Do you like teaching French?"

"I'd much rather be speaking it, as a tourist somewhere."

"Maybe I should just take my chances with the draft," Nat said. "Wonder what they are, my chances."

"You could ask Mother. The statistician."

"But then she'd tell Dad, the good soldier, from a long, long line of good soldiers, that his son's a coward."

"Don't be silly. There are more people against the war than for it." She touched Nat's arm. "It's not cowardly to oppose what you think is wrong. It's the best kind of bravery."

Soon the hemlocks were outnumbered by oaks and

maples. Some hop hornbeam trees. Rhododendrons were beginning to bloom, the mountain laurels not yet. The trail was rocky enough that they had to pay close attention to where they set their feet.

"The problem with starting a hike from Skyline Drive is that it's all downhill from there," she said. "You go down, down, down, and then you're too worn out to hike back up."

"We can turn around anytime you want," Nat said.

"I know. I wasn't complaining."

She asked if he had a girlfriend.

"No one I want to marry. Anyway, that doesn't count as an exemption anymore."

"What about graduate school?"

"I think I'd rather just leave the country. It seems more honest. Is Tim worried about getting drafted?"

"He's twenty-six. So, no."

Nat came to a stop. "Do you think chimpanzees grow up feeling like they have to please their parents? Did we inherit this?"

"Follow your conscience," Gemma said. "Be brave. I could've found a way to get to Paris, but I didn't try hard enough. I'll regret it for the rest of my life."

"Maybe you'll go to France on your honeymoon," Nat said.

Gemma rolled her eyes. "Tim is *very* careful with

his money."

"Doesn't take you to the Crown Sterling for dinner, you mean?"

"While he was in Florida," she said, "his father had a heart attack and had to stop working. Ever since, Tim has been making the mortgage payments for his parents."

"I don't know, Gemma. He's beginning to sound like a keeper. What are his parents like?"

"His father painted houses during the week and preached sermons on Sundays. He can't do ladders anymore, but he's still preaching."

"Uh oh," Nat said. "A preacher for a father-in-law. And his mother?"

"Always in the kitchen, cooking up something for someone."

"Have our parents met his parents?"

"Not yet."

"Then you're not officially engaged." Nat patted her arm, and they continued on down the trail. "What do you like best about him?"

"His eyes," she said. "The way they change color. Completely unrelated to his mood, or what he's think-ing, and so truly magical."

"As if he has hidden depths?"

"Maybe. I never thought of it that way."

There was the distant sound of rushing water.

"The waterfalls, Nat! We're getting close. Don't you just love that sound! Water can go anywhere, anytime it wants."

They stood there listening. It was her favorite place in the world. She was with her very favorite person in the world.

They took their time on the way back up to the hemlock grove, stopping from time to time to catch their breath.

"When I was in Scotland," Nat said, "we spent a few days in the Highlands, and it felt exactly like being in the Appalachians. Same blue mists. No wonder so many Scottish immigrants chose to settle in this area. It must've felt like home."

"Oh, I'd love to go to Scotland."

"And later on, I learned that way back, in pre-history, when all the continents were one big land mass, what are now the Appalachians extended up through Nova Scotia and over to Scotland and on to Scandinavia."

"That gives me chills," Gemma said.

"So, in a way, having grown up here, it wasn't so strange that I felt at home in Scotland."

"Nova Scotia!" she said. "There's your answer."

*   *   *

In June, after Nat had graduated from Georgetown, the two of them spent ten days in Canada, staying in adjacent rooms at a youth hostel in Quebec. Nat had asked for the trip as a graduation present, and, without even asking why he wanted to visit Canada with his sister, their parents obliged.

Cool as cucumbers, Carson and Maryl had been, driving their adult children to the airport in Richmond, giving them hugs on the curb, and saying—cheerfully, and pointedly—"See you back here in two weeks."

It was clear they knew what was up. Their children were running away from home.

A week later, Gemma and Nat were sitting on a bench above the St. Lawrence River—the widest river Gemma had ever seen in her life. Behind them, the setting sun was turning the river to gold.

They'd explored nearly all of Quebec City on foot. That afternoon, they'd even gone horseback riding, in a wooded area with wide dirt trails. Gemma's horse, a sorrel named Lizzy, had three gaits: walk, trot, and run-really-fast (much smoother than a gallop).

Remembering the fourteen-year-old who'd felt transformed after soaring over jumps in the mountains of North Carolina, Gemma felt certain *that* young woman would have found a way to spend a year or two in Paris. While there, she'd surely have been seduced by a French artist and/or writer on a mattress on the floor of an atelier filled with books.

A woman wearing huge sunglasses stopped beside their bench. "Brother and sister?" she chirped.

"No ma'am," Nat drawled. "She's been following me around all day." He turned to Gemma. "Why don't you go with this nice lady here? I bet *she'll* buy you something to eat."

"Don't think so," Gemma said. "Can't ya tell? There's evil eyes behind them fancy shades of hers."

The woman took off her sunglasses and squinted into the sunset. "Americans, right?"

"We work for the CIA," Nat said.

"Funny, you don't look a bit like spies." The woman turned and walked away.

"That's something I've been wanting to tell you." Nat took a deep breath. "I applied for a job with the CIA. I had two semesters of Fortran. My professor wrote a letter of recommendation for me."

"So you'd be working with computers?" she said.

He nodded. "I gave my return address as Lynchburg. Maybe I should call home. See if I have any mail."

Two sailboats were tacking back and forth on the river, as if playing a game of tag. Nat, watching them, spoke softly. "I'll probably never hear back. Except for what I did in class, I have zero programming experience."

"I could call home if you want," Gemma said. "Ask if the school has renewed my teaching contract. If not, then maybe I'll look for a job here."

"I'm loving it here," Nat said. "Are you?"

Gemma nodded. It was her first time, ever, in a foreign country. "You still thinking about staying here? Applying for asylum?"

"It's all I'm thinking about."

"Plus, the CIA."

"That too, yeah."

"Surely, people who work for the CIA don't get drafted. They're already serving their country, just in a different way."

"Exactly. Draft boards refer to them as 'essential civilians.'"

"I bet the CIA will ask you to come for an interview. I bet you'll get the job. If you don't, you can always come back here. Or Toronto. I'll come with you."

"What about Tim?"

"I don't think he'd ever leave his parents. He feels responsible for them."

"So if you marry him, you'll have to live in Buena Vista?"

"Or somewhere close by."

"But you might consider moving to Canada?"

"Maybe."

Nat let out a sigh. "I think I should wait to hear from the CIA. If they don't want me, well then, I'll figure something out."

5

Nat never did hear back from the CIA. He was, however, accepted into a training program for forest rangers in the mountains of western North Carolina—a job Gemma herself would have loved.

And since Nat wouldn't be able to go to Myrtle Beach in August, Gemma decided not to go, either.

"It's where you two met," she reminded her parents. "Isn't it time for a second honeymoon?"

This made her mother smile. "We never really had a first one."

"I thought you were impressed by those ancient Indian mounds in Chillicothe," her father said.

Maryl rolled her eyes.

A few days later, on a steamy Saturday morning in August, Gemma helped her parents load the Datsun.

"It's not too late to change your mind and come with us," her father said.

Gemma shook her head. "I'll be fine here."

"Then behave yourself," he admonished.

"I always have," she replied.

That evening, when Tim rang the doorbell, she asked if he wanted to come in and get cool.

"For a minute, sure. It's awful out here."

"It's OK to kiss me," she said. "My parents have gone to the beach."

"Well, then." Tim leaned down. "Don't mind if I do."

She took his hand, led him up to her bedroom. Twin beds with blue bedspreads. Matching blue tiebacks on the ruffled white curtains.

Gemma lay down on the bed she usually slept in. "There's room for you, too," she said.

"No," Tim said. "We can't."

"Why not? You kiss me. You touch me everywhere. You make me want to, but we're in the VW, where there's not enough room, and you won't lie down with me in the woods because there might be ticks or chiggers or something. Is there something wrong with me?"

Tim shook his head.

"Is it because your father's a preacher?"

Another headshake.

"Then what, Tim? I'd really like to know what's really going on here."

"All right," he said. "All right, Gemma."

Pacing back and forth in front of her chest of drawers, Tim said it had nothing to do with either her or his father and everything to do with a high school girlfriend, whose parents had wanted her to go to college, so they took her somewhere for an abortion, and she died.

"I will never forgive myself," Tim said. "Never. I lost both her and our baby."

Her name was Janie. Tim had wanted to marry her. Her parents said she was too young to be a wife and mother. It would ruin her life.

"She wouldn't have died if they'd just let us get married. They killed her, and they knew it. Some of the responsibility is mine, too, of course. She was only fifteen."

His parents didn't know. Janie's parents had been kind enough not to tell them. After she died, they sold their farm and moved away.

"You can't tell anyone," Tim said. "Ever."

"I won't. I promise."

"I wanted to get it right this time. Marriage first, then sex. I promised myself that, and, back then, I promised God."

She told him she didn't mind waiting, now that she knew.

"I should've told you, Gemma. Instead, I've caused you pain."

"Do I look like her?"

A sad smile from Tim. "She had a blonde ponytail and buck teeth. So, no, Deborah Kerr, you don't."

"It's pronounced Carr. Deborah Carr." Gemma was used to people comparing her to the famous actress in *The King and I.* "And I don't look a bit like her."

"You're beautiful, Gemma. Don't you know that?"

"Mr. Magoo thinks so, too." It was one of Fontana's favorite expressions.

Tim just stared at her.

"You know Mr. Magoo. The near-sighted geezer in the cartoon?"

But Tim shook his head. "Is there a phone up here?"

She led him into her parents' bedroom, where he called his mother. Said Gemma was running a fever, and since her parents were out of town, he was going to stay and take care of her.

"A fever." Gemma couldn't help smiling.

"Is there a drug store open?"

"I just had my period," she said. "I won't get pregnant."

Back in her room, he pushed the two beds together, took off his clothes, and lay down in his underwear.

"Get naked," he said to the ceiling. "I won't watch."

But he did watch.

She lay down beside him, and he began touching her everywhere.

"This is sooo much better than the VW," she whispered.

And then he was on top of her, and it was happening.

Hours later, as the sun was coming up, it happened again.

The following Saturday night, Tim arrived in his father's old painting van. Along the side, in blue script, was the company motto: Let McKenna Do It.

He opened one of the van's back doors. Inside, surrounded by drop cloths, was a mattress.

"Your father's OK with this?" Gemma said.

"If you tell him, I'll never speak to you again. When are your parents coming home?"

"Tomorrow, I think."

Soon they were headed west, toward the mountains, on roads less travelled. After turning onto a dirt road, Tim parked the van beside an ancient, abandoned railroad bridge, its ornate trestles winking in the sunset's glow.

"Beautiful," Gemma said. "How did you know about

this place?"

His eyes changing from blue to gray, Tim smiled at her. "Magic," he said. "Let's climb in back."

Sitting on the mattress, he produced a box of condoms.

"Never used one of these before." He squinted at the instructions. "Sure hope it works."

They got naked. They did it. More than once. It was never just once on that mattress. In the back of the van, in the dark forest, by the silent, empty train tracks, they were free to do whatever they wanted, to cry out if they felt like it, and even to laugh.

They were in love.

A different sort of love than she'd ever felt before, but with an edge of danger.

The reaching out and enfolding, the willingness to trust, had the potential to backfire. A person could fall *in* love, as if it were a deep pit, but then tumble *out* of it, as if from a tall tree.

6

In early December, Tim's father suffered a fatal heart attack. Not long after the funeral, which Gemma attended with her parents, Tim was offered a job in the business office at Washington and Lee University, in Lexington, a short drive from Buena Vista. He continued to live at home, with his mother.

On Saturday nights, he still picked Gemma up in his father's van, still drove her to their spot in the woods beside the railroad trestle. Her parents never asked where the two of them were going, never complained about Gemma's tiptoeing up the stairs to her room very early on Sunday morning. Instead, they seemed to be offering their tacit approval, perhaps hoping that Tim's weekly visits would result in a situation where their long-engaged daughter would finally *have to* get married.

One night in March, Gemma had been dozing in the back of the van when she felt Tim behind her, kissing her neck. "Let's get married in June," he said.

"Ha, ha," Gemma said. "Is this an April Fool's joke?"

"It's time, Gemma. Everyone thinks so. My mother, your mother. Your father has even dropped hint or two."

"Because he wants you to ask for my hand in marriage, so that he can give me away at the altar. I'm not his property, and I won't be yours, either."

"I don't want to own you, Gemma. I want to marry you."

"Why can't we just go on the way we are?"

"Don't you want a house? With our own bed?"

"We could live together, without getting married," Gemma said. "Lots of people do that."

"Like who?"

Fontana for one, wherever she was.

"Don't you want a family?" Tim said.

"Not just yet."

"Well, I do," Tim said. "The sooner the better. I'm tired of seeing you only on Saturdays. I want this every night of the week."

She turned toward him. "Want what?"

"You," he said. "The woman I love."

On Saturday, August 2, 1969—a little more than a week after astronauts had returned from the moon—Gemma and Tim tied the knot, in a ceremony at the Lynchburg church Gemma's parents attended. Gemma had insisted on a very small wedding, with a modest reception at home.

Small because Nat would be there, in his Army uniform, and Gemma was worried she might burst out sobbing at the injustice of it all. Carson, who'd surely known about the draft notice, had said nothing. Not a word to his only son.

Years later, she wouldn't remember saying "I do" at the altar. She would have only a vague memory of the white lace wedding dress her mother had bought for her at a Lynchburg department store. Her clearest memories of the day on which she'd achieved her parents' most important goal for her would be two conversations she'd had at the reception.

After asking her to come outside with him, Nat had told her, in their parents' driveway, that he'd get his orders soon. For Vietnam.

"Can you do something for me, please?" he said softly. "My sense of right and wrong. My conscience. I need to leave them here, with you, where they'll be safe."

He took her right hand, pretended to pour something into it. After she'd closed her hand, he gave her a hug.

That was when she noticed a black-haired woman

in a black dress.

"I heard there was a wedding," Fontana called from the sidewalk.

Her hand still in a fist, Gemma hurried to her friend and gave her a hug. "You got my letter!"

Fontana shook her head. "I'm in town because my grandmother died. Someone at her funeral this morning said you were getting married today. So I thought I'd stop by."

"Grandma Bea died?" Gemma said. "I'm so very sorry."

"You were her favorite, of all my friends." Fontana sighed, turned to Nat. "You've joined the Army?"

"Not by choice," Gemma said. "He got drafted."

"Well, hey!" Fontana said. "I'm flying back to Vancouver tonight. Come with me, Nat. I mean it."

"I can't. That would be desertion." Nat shook his head. "I could get the death penalty."

"Once you're in Canada, you can change your name and disappear," Fontana said. "Hundreds have done it. Thousands."

"I'll fly up there with you," Gemma said.

"But you just got married," Nat said.

"I'll still be married when I get back."

"Newly married and an accessory to a crime on your wedding day. I can't, Gemma. I just can't." He hurried off, his Army shoes clicking on the sidewalk.

"Try not to worry. He'll be OK. Nat always lands on his feet." Fontana gave Gemma a hug. "What's your last name now?"

"McKenna. There's no law that says you have to take your husband's name. But Tim was insulted when I wanted to stay Gemma Sommerset, and so was his mother."

"Gemma Sommerset married Tim McKenna?" Fontana raised her eyebrows, in that way she had. "You're a couple of M&Ms. Will you name your kids Mimi and Max? Marjory and Morris?"

"Kids? I'm not ready for kids. Want to come inside and meet Tim?"

Fontana shook her head, said she wasn't dressed for a wedding.

"Then give me your new address," Gemma said. "Please."

Side by side, dressed in black and white, the long-time friends walked down to where Fontana had parked her mother's blue Buick. Having found a pen, Fontana scribbled an address on an Esso receipt. At the top, Gemma wrote *Fontana Rollins*.

"Unless *you're* planning on getting married," Gemma said.

"I would never change my name for a man," Fontana

said. "Not ever."

"Where's Port Moody?"

"Not far from Vancouver." Fontana shrugged. "I'm with someone else now."

"Another professor?"

"An environmentalist. He wants to move to Alaska."

"Oh!" Gemma said. "I've always wanted to see Alaska! Promise me you'll stay in touch."

"I'll try, Gemma. Really, I will." And Fontana got in the car and drove off.

7

After a short honeymoon at Skyland, in the Shenandoah National Park, Mr. and Mrs. Timothy Robert McKenna moved in with another Mrs. McKenna. Tim's mother, Noreen, was a slender woman who wore her long, gray hair braided and piled on top of her head. The house Tim had grown up in wasn't far from the Buena Vista high school, where he'd been a star football player.

The downstairs of the McKennas' house was one big room, more than half of it taken up by Noreen's all-white kitchen, at one end of which sat an old mahogany table and chairs. Behind the sofa and easy chair to the left of the front door, stairs led up to two bedrooms and a full bath.

In Tim's bedroom, Gemma helped him push the twin beds together. "Just like our first time," she joked. "And almost as dangerous." Weary of condoms and wary of the new birth control pills, she'd decided to take her chances.

Tim put a finger to his lips. "You'll have to be quiet.

Despite her age, my mother has excellent hearing."

Noreen was also an excellent cook. When she realized how little Gemma knew about meal preparation, she offered to teach her how to make some of Tim's favorite dishes.

"That's very kind of you," Gemma said. "My mother always did the cooking. I'm pretty good at setting the table and washing dishes."

Noreen gave her a look. "So is Tim."

Having finally parted with his VW, Tim drove off each morning, to his job in nearby Lexington, in a 1969 white Chevy Impala. Gemma would usually help Noreen with the breakfast dishes and then go out for a walk. A very long walk around aptly named Buena Vista, whose hazy mountain views reminded her that these very same mountains extended southward, into North Carolina, where she'd once gone horseback riding early on a Sunday morning.

She couldn't help wondering: what would that Gemma think of this one?

This one could speak French—had even taught it. But had she ever traveled to Paris? Did she have the master's degree she'd once felt destined for? No and no.

Instead, still in Virginia, at age twenty-six, she'd married the only man she'd ever "gone steady" with.

They were now living in his mother's house, where the reading material, arranged haphazardly in a bookcase beside the stove, consisted of cookbooks, phone books, and an old Webster's dictionary.

They'd been married for two and a half weeks when disaster struck.

Noreen, a huge fan of TV weather forecasts, had warned them. At dinner that night, she'd said that Hurricane Camille, two days after having made landfall in Mississippi, was headed their way.

"Nothing to worry about, though," she said. "They say that once it's crossed over the mountains, the storm will lose strength. We'll get a lot of rain, that's all."

Instead, the torrential rains and high winds kept them awake all night. There was a constant roaring sound, as if a train were passing overhead. With a loud pop, the electricity went out.

The next morning, Buena Vista resembled a lake. Tim's car and his mother's had both been swept away. The basement was completely flooded, the first floor under nearly a foot of water.

The whole town reeked of mud and slime. It stank to high heaven, as Nat would've put it.

No electricity. No running water.

"Not sure it's safe to stay here," Tim said.

"But where can we go?" Gemma said. "How would we get there?"

Weeping, Noreen scavenged for edible food in the dark refrigerator. The three of them ate together at a small table in her bedroom.

"This wasn't supposed to happen," she kept saying. "How could they have been so completely wrong?"

"It's why they're called weather 'predictions,'" Tim said. "'Chance of rain,' they'll say. It's like gambling. Playing the odds."

"But they usually get it right," Noreen wailed. "Folks will be expecting me to bring them food. They count on me."

"No one will expect that, Mother," Tim insisted. "No one. You're not a magician."

Two days later, Noreen was downstairs when someone began pounding on the front door. She opened the door, then called upstairs.

"Gemma! Your father's here!"

Gemma was still in her nightgown. Hadn't combed her hair. No matter. She ran down the stairs, threw her arms around her father.

"We've been so very worried about you," he said.

"Was it bad in Lynchburg?" she said. "Is Mother OK?"

"We got some rain. But nothing like this." He took a breath. "It's even worse here than I imagined it would be."

"A disaster zone," Tim said from the top of the stairs. "But we're OK."

"Thank the Good Lord," Noreen said.

"I want you to come back to Lynchburg with me," Carson said. "All three of you. You can catch your breath there. Figure out what to do next."

It took Tim several hours to convince his mother to leave her home of more than thirty years. "It's only temporary," he kept saying. "Till things get better here."

Finally, Noreen packed some clothing. Into a cardboard box went her favorite cookbooks, the most crucial utensils, the best pots and pans.

That night, a Lynchburg weatherman insisted that even the climate scientists couldn't explain why and how it all happened. Instead of weakening after crossing the Appalachians, Camille had somehow intensified, causing the usually tame Maury River, in Buena

Vista, to become a wall of water thirty feet high.

"I just can't believe it," Noreen kept saying.

"She's still in shock," Carson whispered to Gemma.

But Tim knew what to do. After a private phone conversation with his sister, Louise, in Tallahassee, he handed his mother the phone.

"No," Noreen kept saying to her daughter. "Thank you, but I just can't. You have no idea what I've been through."

The next day, when the two of them spoke again, Noreen had softened. "Well, maybe for just a short visit. A change of scenery might help."

A few days later, she was on a plane to Florida.

"One reason she decided to go," Tim admitted to Gemma, "was that she needs to be in charge in the kitchen. Louise knows that and doesn't mind."

"My mother wouldn't have minded, if she'd known," Gemma said.

"It's better this way," Tim said. "I'll deal with HUD. Not sure she's up to negotiating with bureaucrats."

So that he could return to his job at Washington and Lee, which was an hour's drive from Lynchburg, Tim rented a car. Occasionally, he spent the night in Lexington so that he could check on his mother's house. Buena Vista was still in shambles, he reported. They weren't the only ones who'd left town.

"You married a good man," Gemma's father said to her one night. "I'm proud to be his father-in-law."

"I thought you'd had reservations about Tim," Gemma said.

"Parents always worry. You'll see."

And yet he didn't seem to be the least bit worried about Nat, who was in Kentucky, awaiting orders for Vietnam.

Hurricanes came and went. Wars lasted for decades.

Gemma knew it in her gut. Their father could've come to Nat's rescue, too.

8

At age twenty-six, Gemma Sommerset McKenna, married for less than a month, had left her mother-in-law's house and, with her husband, moved back in with her parents. That she was once again sleeping in her childhood bed felt like the opposite of progress.

In October, she learned she was pregnant.

Tim was happy. Her parents were happy. Gemma claimed to be excited and most days she was. She also worried that she wasn't ready, just yet, to be a mother. She knew nothing at all about babies.

And where they would they live? Tim was already tired of his daily commute from Lynchburg to Lexington. His mother's house in Buena Vista was uninhabitable.

He refused to waste money on rent.

So, the newlyweds/expectant parents went house-hunting.

What sort of house were they looking for? the real

estate agent in Lexington cheerfully asked.

Gemma was hoping for mountain views, Tim a ground-floor office with an outside entrance for private clients.

The next day, the agent said she was so very sorry. There were no properties like that in their price range.

She showed them several houses in an older neighborhood with a mix of large, historic houses and newer, smaller ones. Many of the streets sloped down to the Woods Creek Trail leading to Washington and Lee University. An excellent location, she pointed out, which would allow Tim to walk to work and Gemma to have his new car (another Impala, this one moss-green) during the day.

The Impala nearly matched the third house they looked at, a two-story with green siding and white trim. In the side yard were a sycamore and an oak, magnificent trees, far older than the house itself.

While leading them up the stairs, the agent gestured grandly at the rooms along the back of the house. "Your second and third bedrooms," she chirped, "with a full bath between them."

In the larger of these rooms, she gave Gemma a conspiratorial smile. "Won't this make a lovely nursery?"

"Not sure the other room is big enough for my office," Tim said.

"What about using the dining room as your office?" the agent said.

"I need to be able to close a door," Tim said. "Financial clients want, and deserve, their privacy."

Standing at the large window in the possible nursery, Gemma could see the oak and sycamore to her left. Straight ahead, beyond a brick wall, was a slate-roofed cottage.

"I'm facing east, right?" Gemma said.

"Pretty much," the agent said. "Ready to see the master bedroom?"

They followed her down the hall.

"And look!" The woman gestured. "You'll have your very own master bath!"

"For him?" Gemma said.

"For both of you. Check it out. It's really quite large."

"So," Gemma said, "big enough for the master *and* his mistress."

"Please excuse her," Tim said. "It's her first pregnancy."

Gemma wasn't finished. "Does this terminology date back to slavery?"

Looking confused, the woman shook her head.

"He's not my master." Gemma motioned to Tim. "Do you think of your own husband that way?"

"Gemma," Tim cautioned. "It's just real estate speak."

"Words have meanings. A master bedroom implies that there's a master. Ditto for a master bath."

"You know," the agent snapped. "I don't have to sell you this house."

But she did.

I'm about to become a mother with a mortgage, Gemma wrote to Fontana in November. We're buying a house in Lexington, not far from where Tim works. Baby due in June. Here's my new address. Please, PLEASE write back to me pronto, OK? Happy Thanksgiving!

The shorter the note, she figured, the more likely Fontana would be to respond.

9

In December, Nat flew off to Vietnam. Having written two letters home, he didn't bother with (or perhaps couldn't find) a Christmas card.

On January 3, 1970, the US Army informed his parents that Nathanial Owings Sommerset was missing in action.

When their father called Gemma with the news, his voice broke. He wasn't the kind of man to cry.

Close to tears herself, she managed not to remind him it was all his fault. Refrained from pointing out that their family's proud history of military service should have ended with Nat's birth, not his (probable) death. For months, she avoided speaking to her father at all.

Which wasn't fair, and she knew it. Yes, he bore some of the responsibility, but the person *really* at fault was Nat's namby-pamby sister. Who should have encouraged her courageous brother to stay in Quebec. Should've stayed there with him, at least until he'd found a job, and friends he could rely on.

Instead, she had failed her only sibling.

What had happened to the fearless girl who'd soared over high jumps on a mountain trail? The fourteen-year-old who'd been so certain that, for the rest of her life, she'd be capable of meeting all challenges?

On good days, Gemma reminded herself that Nat was an expert hiker. Fully capable of making his way through Laos or Cambodia and ending up in Thailand. She imagined him staying with friends in Bangkok. Nat had always made friends so easily.

Most days, she knew that she would never, ever see her brother again.

10

His name would've been Nat, if they'd had a boy. Instead, in June of 1970, Gemma and Tim McKenna became the parents of a baby girl, Noreen. Her namesake was still in Florida, waiting for the house in Buena Vista to be made livable again.

One night, Gemma was awakened, in the room she shared with her husband, by an especially loud wailing. Careful not to disturb Tim, who kept insisting that his job required him to be alert during the day, she rolled out of bed, hurried down the hall, and turned on the light in the nursery.

Tiny Noreen lay on her back, kicking and screaming and red as a beet, her diaper leaking liquid poop onto the crib sheet. After Gemma had changed and disposed of the diaper, the new one quickly filled up again. She set her tiny, stinky daughter in one corner of the bed and began removing the sheet.

Having changed the diaper yet again, Gemma bundled all the soiled items together, intending to carry them and Noreen into the bathroom. But simply picking Noreen up resulted in grand arcs of vomit landing on the pale green curtains patterned with Raggedy Ann and Andy dolls. Gemma's mother had found the material and sewn the curtains herself.

Projectile vomiting (a term Gemma would soon add to her vocabulary). Little Noreen could have won Olympic gold in projectile vomiting.

In the bathroom between the nursery and Tim's office, Gemma tossed the soiled nightgown and sheets into the tub. She sponged Noreen off, fastened her into a new diaper, wrapped her in a towel, and sat down with her on the toilet.

"What's wrong?" she whispered.

And Noreen smiled.

Gemma sat waiting for this mysterious creature to burp, or pass gas, or worse. But Noreen, still smiling, dozed off.

Instead of going in search of clean crib sheets, Gemma just sat there, on the toilet, in the stinky bathroom, with her tiny daughter asleep in her lap. She wondered if her own mother had had nights like this, those many years ago, in Columbus, Ohio—up all night with a leaky baby girl whose father was somewhere in Europe, fighting the Nazis.

Through the bathroom's tiny window, Gemma caught a glimpse of pale lilac. A new day was dawning.

Using great care, she was able to stand without waking her precious cargo. She then carried Noreen back to the crib and covered her with a clean blanket.

Slowly, quietly, she opened the vomit-stained curtains. And was greeted by a glorious, fiery-orange sky. A precious gift, addressed to her, from the universe, or so it seemed. Her very own personal reward.

As the new day dawned, Gemma realized she was smiling. Feeling a little more comfortable with the whole motherhood thing.

The curtains shrank in the wash—perhaps they should have been dry-cleaned. Gemma didn't bother replacing them.

Each morning, awakened by an internal clock, she would quietly leave the bed she shared with Tim and go down to the kitchen. Brew a pot of coffee. Leave boxes of cereal and a bowl and a spoon on the counter. A loaf of bread. Tim knew where to find the milk, how to use the toaster.

Mug of coffee in hand, she would then climb the stairs, tiptoe into her daughter's room, and sit down, facing the bare window, in the rocking chair that had belonged to her mother's mother. Even on cloudy days she did this, being ever so careful not to wake

Noreen up.

"There are no guarantees in this life," her father often said. "Nothing lasts forever."

But the sun was always there, always had been, always would be. No wonder so many ancient civilizations had worshipped it.

"Mommy," Noreen whined one morning. "You woke me up." She was four years old.

"Go back to sleep, then," Gemma said. "I'm just sitting here, being very quiet, as usual."

"Can't you be quiet in your own room?" Noreen said.

"It's not the same. I can't watch the sun come up from there."

"But this is my room, Mommy. You belong in Daddy's room. Not mine."

"So, you have a room, and Daddy has a room, and I don't?"

Noreen thought this over. "You and Daddy have a room. And this is my room."

"I thought you didn't mind if I came to your room in the morning."

"Daddy says you're addicted to sunrise."

"He told you that?"

Noreen gave a solemn nod.

"What does 'addicted' mean," Gemma asked. "Do you know?"

"Beats the shit out of me."

"Noreen! Who says that?"

"Susie's dad. He says it all the time."

Gemma finished her coffee. "I'll make a deal with you. I'll stop coming to your room in the morning, if you'll stop repeating what Susie's dad says."

"Deal," Noreen said.

"The thing is, though, I really do need to watch the sun come up."

"Why?" Noreen said.

How could she explain her obsession to a preschooler? "The way the sky changes color makes me feel hopeful," she said.

Noreen nodded, as if she completely understood. Then she wrinkled her nose. "I don't like the sun. It wakes me up."

"Then maybe we should get new curtains," Gemma said.

"What happened to the old ones?"

"One night, when you were a little baby, you threw up all over them."

"I did not."

"You couldn't help it," Gemma said. "You were very sick. And then the sun appeared, and I knew everything was going to be OK."

"I'm a big girl now. I need my sleep."

"All right. Then what kind of curtains should we get?"

"Lots of colors, like a box of crayons."

Like the sky at sunrise, Gemma thought. "I'll tell your Grandmama. Maybe she can find something like that in Lynchburg."

"I better go with her," Noreen said. "So she'll get it right."

11

In the third bedroom, the windows facing east were almost completely blocked by Tim's file cabinets. Still, his office was better for sunrise-watching than the back porch.

It was after he'd begun scheduling weekend clients that Gemma had her brilliant idea.

When one of these clients, Caleb, the carpenter, came down the stairs from Tim's office on a Saturday afternoon, Gemma asked Caleb if he might be interested in building a deck for them. Wearing his usual black T-shirt, which matched his shoulder-length, curly black hair, Caleb followed her out the back door.

"I want to be able to watch the sun rise," she explained. "Tim thinks I can do that from here on the porch, but . . ." She gestured toward the neighbors' house, the mature trees. "I need to be higher up."

"For sure." Caleb pointed east. "I live over on the edge of town. Best part of my day, watching the sun peek over the mountains."

"The mountains! Oh, I'd love to be able to do that!"

Caleb suggested adding a third story to their house, with a roof deck. Tim could have a larger office up there, and she'd be able to see the sun rise over the Blue Ridge. "A win-win," he said.

Gemma loved the idea. Tim nixed it. Too expensive.

"If you feel the need to watch the sun come up over the mountains," he said to Gemma, "then just get in the car."

"I want to see it from here," she said. "In my nightgown. While drinking coffee."

Insisting that a nice deck would increase their property value, Caleb drew up plans for replacing the back porch roof with a deck running the length of the house. A new door would provide access to the deck from Tim's office. In nice weather, he could meet with his clients outside.

Tim didn't want a door. He also vetoed a door to the deck from Noreen's room. Said it wouldn't be long before she might be tempted, like Juliet, to run off with some Romeo. Or, even worse, invite said Romeo into her room.

He even objected to a flight of steps from the back porch to the deck. A burglar might climb up and break in through one of the windows.

"Then how would I get to the deck?" Gemma said. "Levitate? A smart burglar would break in downstairs, while we're asleep."

Caleb backed her up. "This is Lexington, Virginia, not some crime-ridden metropolis."

Together, they wore Tim down.

Gemma was watching that morning, as Caleb gripped the railing on the new deck, testing its strength. Tim was at work, Noreen now at school.

"Final inspection," Caleb said. "Don't want anyone to fall off. Tim would sue me from here to kingdom come."

"Not to worry. I'll be up here alone, sitting in a chair, with a thermos of coffee, waiting for sunrise. This is a dream come true, Caleb, really it is."

"Thought about trying to build a sort of lifeguard chair, so you could climb up and maybe see the mountains. But I worried about you doing that in the dark."

"That's sweet of you." She touched his arm. "You'll have to come over some morning and watch with me."

He shook his head. "I'm engaged."

"Jeez, Caleb, I wasn't coming on to you."

They waited for the awkward moment to pass.

"Maybe we should add a floodlight?" He said this

softly, gesturing toward the steps.

"A floodlight might spoil things."

"We don't want to spoil things," he said.

"No," she said.

They stood in silence, their hands nearly touching on the railing.

"You know," he said, "the sun comes up in different places each morning, depending on what time of year it is."

"I do know that. The ancient Egyptians did, too."

"The analemma," he said.

"Yes!" She motioned toward the oak and the sycamore in the side yard. "In winter, you see sunrise through their branches."

"And now? Were you up here this morning?"

"I was!" She pointed straight ahead.

"Maybe I *will* drop by some morning," Caleb said.

"The clover." She pointed down. "Underneath this part of the deck. Will it die, now that it doesn't get any sunlight?"

"Don't know. Does it matter?"

"I found a four-leaf clover last summer," she said. "Three of them, in fact."

"I'm never that lucky."

"Maybe I could find one for you."

He followed her down the steps. Under the deck, he

took her arm, led her deeper into the shade.

"I've been wanting, for so long, to touch you," he said.

"I had no idea."

"Sure you did. Isn't that why we're down here where no one can see us?"

"I thought I was going to try to find you a four-leaf clover."

"Do I need one?" He touched her cheek, then leaned down and kissed her.

She kissed him back.

"I'm moving to Bristol, in June, to get married," he said. "Bristol's where we'll live."

"Got it," she said. "I hope you'll be very happy."

"I'm happy right now." He began unbuttoning her dress, then helped her step out of her panties. "Never been so happy in my whole dang life."

She watched him take off his boots, his jeans.

"You're on the pill?" he said.

She nodded. A reckless, indefensible lie. She'd been trying for years to get pregnant again. With a boy this time, whose name would be Nat.

"Here?" Caleb pressed her against the dining room wall.

"No," she said. "In the clover."

In the clover, she wrapped her legs around him, tried

not to cry out.

"Jesus," he moaned. "Lord God in Heaven."

And then Caleb was gone.

A little later, in a daze, she hung the dress she'd been wearing—a blue-plaid madras shirtwaist—at the back of her closet. A constant reminder, on a wooden hanger, of the person she really was.

Part II

Secrets and Surprises

12

On her first night at the hotel, Gemma was brushing her teeth when she heard a loud boom. Next thing she knew, she was standing beside the bed.

She made her way to the window and yanked open the curtains, expecting to see panic and pointing and yelling down below. But the street and the sidewalks were empty.

She waited for the wail of sirens.

Nothing.

So, she closed the curtains, chalked it up to a long travel day, finished brushing her teeth, and went to bed.

This was in Carmel, California. May, 1990.

The following morning, in the hotel restaurant, the family at the table next to hers were talking about the earthquake. By listening in, Gemma was able to verify that, yes, on her very first night in California, she had indeed experienced an earthquake.

Good omen or bad?

For her trip to California, the farthest she'd ever

been from home, she'd had new business cards printed up. Against a background of pale orange clouds, the cards announced:

Gemma Sommerset, Travel Writer
Lexington, Virginia

From the beginning, Tim had been less than enthusiastic about her so-called career. Could not understand why she would even want to work. Kept reminding her that he made more than enough money to support the three of them.

His mother hadn't ever had to work. And neither had Gemma's.

It's not for the money, she'd given up trying to explain. Tim was well aware of the fact that she rarely cleared expenses.

Her first travel article had happened almost by accident. While Tim was attending an accountants' convention in New York, Gemma had wandered around Manhattan on her own, a delicious sort of freedom. They'd left six-year-old Noreen in Lynchburg, with Gemma's parents.

Somewhere near Chinatown, Gemma noticed a store called Liberated and stopped to peer in through the dusty shop windows. Remembering the camera her father had "liberated" from the Germans, she ventured inside.

The shop had a musty smell. Its glass display cases were labeled: Revolutionary War, Civil War, World War I, World War II, etc. Avoiding the cases of memorabilia from Vietnam, Gemma saw that there were indeed German cameras, from both world wars. There were muskets and cannonballs, swords and helmets. A few Mussolini and Hitler posters.

"What are you looking for?" demanded the shopkeeper, a bald Asian man.

"I'm a writer," Gemma lied. "I think visitors to New York would be interested in your shop."

The man shrugged.

She took a pen and Tim's convention schedule from her pocketbook and, in the margins, began listing some of the items for sale.

"I don't see any prices," she said.

"Negotiable," came the reply.

She continued taking notes, then asked the price of a Confederate $2 bill.

"Two dollars seem fair?"

"Fair and square," she said.

"Must remember that." He winked at her. "Fair and square."

Back home in Virginia, she consulted her scribbles and wrote a few pages about her visit to Liberated. She then enclosed the pages with a note thanking her parents for taking care of Noreen.

Her father, who was still teaching high school English, had begun writing a weekly column for the *Lynchburg News and Advance*. He called her to ask if he could make a few changes to the article and see if the newspaper would publish it.

The newspaper did.

Her next article sold to the Travel Section of the *Baltimore Sun*. That one was about the George Washington National Forest, not far from Lexington. Gemma could wander the trails and talk to the forest rangers and be home by the time Noreen's school let out. She felt mesmerized by the trees, soothed by their eternal silence.

During October—deer hunting season—she stayed home.

Fascinated by forests, she branched out—Tim's little joke—making weekend trips to West Virginia, Maryland, and even Kentucky. Her article comparing the Daniel Boone National Forest near Lexington, Kentucky, with its counterpart near Lexington, Virginia, had sold to *Southern Living*, after *National Geographic* of course turned it down.

"Into the forest I go, to lose my mind and find my soul." T-shirts attributed the quote to John Muir. It sure sounded like Muir. But when Gemma had contacted the Sierra Club to ask for the exact source, they'd replied that they were unable to verify that John Muir had ever said those words.

In 1988, there had been heartbreaking news: an invasion of the Shenandoah National Park by the hemlock woolly adelgid, which threatened to destroy the historic hemlock grove in the Limberlost. The magnificent trees she and Nat had visited, time and time again, were being killed by a tiny, invasive insect.

Gemma got right to work. Amazingly, the *Washington Post* published her plea that readers visit the magnificent, old-growth hemlocks while the trees were still standing.

The *Post* article was a feather in her cap. It was also her last attempt to write about living trees, whose future on this planet had begun to seem as uncertain as that of any other life form.

Instead, in what seemed even to her a perverse move, she decided to write about dead trees.

Having read, somewhere, that several famous poets had written their poems in secluded log cabins, she decided to embark—from the French "embarquer," meaning "to board a (wooden) ship"—on a series of articles about solitary artists whose creative processes involved staring at, or pacing back and forth on, former trees.

John Muir's log cabin in Yosemite was no longer standing, but Robert Frost's, in Ripton, Vermont, was still intact. As was the log cabin in Dawson City, in Canada's Yukon, where Robert Service had penned his verses. Joaquin Miller had written in a log cabin in Rock Creek Park, in Washington, DC. Robinson Jeffers and his wife had lived in a log cabin in Carmel.

DC would have been the closest. But with Noreen away at college already, Gemma had been eager to do some real traveling. Fly all the way to the other side of the country. Wade into a brand-new ocean.

She'd waited until tax season was over. With an increasing number of private clients, Tim counted on her to answer the phone, keep his appointments calendar, and serve coffee or tea if anyone wanted it. For years, she'd been his unpaid assistant. This year, he would pay for her round-trip flight to Carmel and five nights in a hotel.

The morning after the earthquake, she left her hotel, map in hand, and went to see if Carmel's public library was open on Sundays. The white, Spanish-style building, with its tall, arched windows, was as picturesque as the rest of the town. Out front, flowers were blooming. The sign on the door said the library would be open from noon to four.

It was a cool, sunny morning. Carmel, she already knew, was an easily walkable town, one square mile in area, divided into a neat grid of streets and avenues. Its small lots had once been tent sites for refugees—many of them artists—from the 1906 San Francisco earthquake. Eventually, the tents were replaced by small cottages, their architectural styles ranging from English fairytale to mission, art deco to Craftsman. Most of the current owners of these cottages were millionaires.

Nearly every article she'd read about Carmel had described the town in exactly this way. She intended to write about one log cabin and the poet who'd been inspired to write there.

By eleven a.m., two o'clock Virginia time, she was more than ready for lunch. From Ocean Avenue, she turned onto Casanova Street, where Carson's Café, a white brick cottage with blue trim, caught her eye.

The waiter, a wiry man with a deep voice and curly brown hair, looked to be in his forties. Gemma ordered artichoke soup and a shrimp and avocado salad.

"Coming right up," he said. "Where y'all from?"

"Virginia. Can you tell?"

"Don't worry," he said. "Carmel's a very friendly place. You'll see."

"Do you live here? In Carmel, I mean."

"Do I look like a millionaire?" He rolled his eyes.

After leaving the café, she walked to the library. Inside, real logs were burning in an actual fireplace, in front of which were a large sofa and a group of easy chairs. All seats were taken, their occupants either reading or dozing.

A petite librarian in a blue-and-white, Scandinavian-style sweater widened her eyes at Gemma's question. "Follow me," she said.

In the local history section, the librarian took down a few books and set them on a table. She opened one and pointed to a photo.

"As you can see," she said, "the Jeffers cabin is, quite literally, falling apart. No one lives there. No one will even buy it."

"But Robinson Jeffers wrote poetry there?"

"Maybe a little. But you'll want to go to Tor House."

"What's that?" Gemma said.

"It's the beautiful stone house Jeffers and his wife built, overlooking the ocean. *That's* where he wrote almost all his poetry."

Gemma felt sick. If Robinson Jeffers had done his

best work not in a log cabin but in a house made of stone, then she'd come all the way to California for nothing.

Perhaps sensing her disappointment, the librarian added, "The cabin's only a few blocks from here. Monte Verde Avenue and Fourth Street. If you want, you can walk over and see for yourself."

Gemma wrote the address in her notebook. She thanked the librarian and took down more books, hoping to come across a nugget of information which might salvage her trip.

One book reminded her that the Spanish were in California long before the Pilgrims arrived at Plymouth Rock. Hoping some detail would catch her eye—an early Spanish explorer, perhaps, who'd composed poems in a primitive cabin beside the Pacific—she kept turning pages.

When one of the easy chairs was vacated, she moved over to sit by the fire. A man in a blue plaid shirt glanced up at her, then went back to his book. *Speak Memory,* by Vladimir Nabokov.

And it occurred to her that Carmel's present-day residents might be more interesting than the Spanish settlers. The librarian, for one. Could she afford to live in town? If not, did she have a long commute to work? Was that a problem for her and her family? Would she mind answering such very personal questions?

Instead of trying to find the dilapidated cabin she'd come all the way across the country to see, Gemma decided to remain by the fire, surreptitiously observing the locals on a Sunday afternoon. She also decided not to tell Tim, who'd always resented her "little trips," about the sloppy research for her first big trip.

When the man in the blue plaid shirt closed his book, stood up, and left the library, no alarm went off. Wondering if *Speak Memory* was already checked out, Gemma nearly followed him outside to ask.

Soon a bell dinged, signifying that the library was closing. She gathered up the books she'd skimmed through and placed them on a book cart. Looked, in vain, for the librarian and then headed outside.

It was a gorgeous afternoon in late May, in unbearably picturesque Carmel. Whose full name, Gemma remembered, was Carmel-by-the-Sea.

She hadn't seen an ocean in years.

13

Returning to Ocean Avenue, she followed it west, toward the Pacific, the same ocean that had made her father so very seasick on his trips to and from Japan. The ocean Nat had flown over in 1969.

At the end of Ocean Avenue, ancient cypress trees, silhouetted against the horizon, leaned permanently leeward, their ancient limbs gnarled and disfigured from an eternal struggle with the wind. Gemma felt certain the trees had been there when the Spanish arrived.

She placed her hand on one of trunks, wishing the cypress could share its many secrets with her. Then she looked down.

And there—far, far below—was the Pacific Ocean.

On the east coast, beaches were only a few steps down from the road. To get to Carmel's beach she would have to descend one wooden staircase after another.

There were people down there, walking along the sand or sitting in beach chairs. Even dogs had managed the multiple flights of steps.

With one last look at the ancient cypresses, down she went.

While standing at the ocean's edge, looking out at the horizon, it hit her that Pacific was entirely the wrong name for this ocean she associated with war. Two wars.

Her father, after having written numerous letters from Japan, had come home. Her brother had written twice from Viet Nam and disappeared.

Was Vietnam due west of California? Someone claiming to be a travel writer should know a basic detail like that.

Hovering in the near distance was Nat's face.

This happened sometimes. She would feel his presence, his concern for her, his forgiveness. But then he would disappear.

She took a few steps back, sat down on the sand, and untied her sneakers. Removed a sock and used it to dab at her eyes. While she was taking off the other sock, a Dalmatian bounded up.

"Sit, Gorgeous!" a male voice barked.

It was the man from the library, in the blue plaid shirt.

Obediently, Gorgeous sat.

You look so sad, Carson had said to Maryl on the pier in Myrtle Beach.

"Is something wrong?" this man said.

Gemma shook her head.

"Don't I know you?" he said.

The world's oldest pickup line. She answered him anyway. "I was at the library. You were reading Nabokov."

"Ah," he said vaguely.

"'The spiral is a circle that has been set free.'"

He frowned, looking confused. Gorgeous had wandered off.

"A quote from *Speak Memory,*" she said.

"A paraphrase, maybe, not a direct quote."

"Maybe."

"I'm Logan."

"Gemma." She stuffed her socks into her shoes and stood up. No one else was in the water—no swimmers, no waders, not even an adventuresome dog.

"You must be a tourist," he said. "I'll guard your shoes. Better keep your purse with you, though. You don't know me from Adam."

She rolled up her slacks, shouldered her pocketbook, and splashed into the ocean. Which was freezing cold, numbingly so. Stubbornly, she kept going, until an insistent wave convinced her otherwise. On feet she could no longer feel, she made her way back to the dry sand, where Logan was sitting beside her sneakers.

"No wonder no one's swimming," she said.

"August is when people swim. Will you be here then?"

She shook her head.

"You like Nabokov?"

Shivering, she bit her lips and nodded.

His smile reminded her of toothpaste ads, the teeth very white, perhaps artificially so. His hair was not white, not yet. He was wearing an intricately carved gold wedding ring.

Gorgeous bounded up, and Logan got to his feet. Walking off with her shoes and socks, he headed south along the sand.

"Better come with me," he called over his shoulder. "You don't even have a towel."

It felt a little like giving a horse its head.

Attached to a narrow set of wooden steps shaded by pine trees, a weathered sign warned: *Private Property*. Before bounding up the steps, Gorgeous allowed her owner to wipe the sand from her paws with a gray towel.

"Do you want to come up?" Logan said. "Or, I can

bring a clean towel down for you."

"I'll use that one." Gemma held out her hand.

"No, you won't." Carrying her shoes and socks, he followed Gorgeous up the steps.

Holding on to the railing, she spent some time brushing sand from first one damp foot and then the other. Then she started up.

At the top of the steps was a wooden deck attached to a stone cottage. Logan and Gorgeous had disappeared. To the left of a sliding glass door, beside a stack of firewood, were her shoes and socks.

She sat down on a lounge chair, from which she could see the ocean through the trees. Thought about asking this man and his wife how often they watched the sun set over the ocean, then putting the same question to the waiter and the librarian. "Those Who Live in Carmel and Those Who Serve the Ones Who Do" might be too long for a title but was perfect for her article's theme.

Logan reappeared with a fluffy peach bath towel. Having dried her feet, Gemma was putting on her socks and shoes when he returned with two cups of tea.

"Put a wee drop of brandy in mine," he said. "That sound good to you?"

She nodded, placing the cup on a small table beside

her chair.

He went back inside, returned with a bottle of brandy, dribbled some into her tea.

"You could wrap yourself in the towel and let me put your slacks in the dryer," he said. "They'll be dry in no time."

"I'll just sit here in the sun," she said.

"What was that quote again?" he said. "From Nabokov."

"The spiral is a circle that has been set free."

"I think that's the gist of it, yes." He set his cup down, went back inside, and returned with *Speak Memory*. Then, seated in the lounge chair next to hers, he riffled the pages. "It begins a chapter."

"You have a photographic memory?"

"I can sometimes remember where something is on a page. Yes, here it is. Chapter Fourteen. 'The spiral is a spiritualized circle. In the spiral form, the circle, uncoiled, unwound, has ceased to be vicious. It has been set free.'"

"May I see?" She held out her hand.

The book had no call number on the spine, no library bar code on the back. "I did have the gist of it," she said.

"The very essence."

They sat staring out at the ocean. An oddly comfortable silence.

"How long have you lived here?" she asked.

"A while," he replied.

A real travel writer would've prompted him for more. Gemma simply nodded.

"Guess I should be getting back," she said then. A bald-faced lie. No one was expecting her. She had no plans, for this evening or even for the rest of the week. "May I use your bathroom before I go?"

He stood up, opened the sliding glass door, and pointed. "At the top of the stairs. The clothes dryer's up there, too."

She stepped into a room with a slate-tiled floor. Three walls held floor-to-ceiling bookshelves—hundreds of books. At the far end of the room, beside the stairs, was a fireplace. Through the window beside the front door, she glimpsed a garden.

There was no sign of a wife.

She wondered why a man with an extensive library, and a fireplace of his own, would go to a library to read one of his very own books by the fire.

Upstairs, the flooring was pine. The washer and dryer were next to the bathroom. After wrapping herself in another fluffy peach towel, she put her slacks and panties in the dryer, then tiptoed into the larger of the two bedrooms. Heavy oak furniture. A dark green quilted bedspread covering a king-size bed.

Later, her clothes dry, she found Logan in the kitchen. He opened a cabinet, turned toward her. "If you'd like, we could have pasta for dinner."

"All right," she said. "Can I help?"

He poured two glasses of wine, handed her one of them. Took a plastic container from the freezer. "I can warm this up all by myself. I'm even good at boiling water. Go sit down. Make yourself at home."

She wondered if he'd noticed *her* wedding ring. He didn't seem interested in where she was from, what she was doing in Carmel, how long she was planning to stay. Was this a millionaire's mindset? The current moment is what matters; allow it to spiral into whatever comes next.

Seated on the sofa, sipping her wine, she noticed a book of poems on the coffee table. *You Can't Have Everything,* by Richard Shelton. She picked it up and read a few of the poems with checkmarks in pencil beside their titles: "Local Knowledge," "Comfort," "Letter to a Dead Father," "Whatever Became of Me."

Eerily beautiful despair, in the Sonoran Desert.

It had become too chilly to sit on the deck, so they ate at the redwood picnic table in the kitchen.

"I've never seen so many books," she said. "In a private home, I mean."

"A lot of them belonged to my grandfather," he said.

"Like Richard Shelton's poems?"

"No, those books are mine. Shelton's one of my favorites." He stood up, carried their dishes to the sink, and left the kitchen. Returning with two windbreakers, he gave her one of them.

"For dessert, shall we watch the sun set?"

She followed him out to the deck and stood next to him at the railing. Through the pines, the sky appeared to be on fire. Gemma had the words on her tongue—*do you live here alone?*—when he told her his wife was in San Francisco. "Her mother had a stroke."

Knowing the polite response would be *I'm sorry*, she said it.

He kissed her, tasting of oregano, and she kissed him back.

"Would you like to stay for the night?" he said.

"I should call my hotel. See if there are any messages." She did, after all, have aging parents. A daughter away at college. A husband who might call with bad news about one or all of them.

"The phone's in the kitchen," he said. "I'm going to take Gorgeous out."

* * *

The hotel said she had no messages. Not a single reason to abandon this kind, intelligent man who wanted her to spend the night.

She was sitting on the sofa, lit by the sunset's final splendor, when Logan and Gorgeous returned. Logan sat down beside her. Gorgeous settled beside the fireplace.

"You can stay?" he said.

"How long have you lived here?" she said.

"Oh, let's not ruin this. Talking gets people absolutely nowhere."

But I don't even know you, she wanted to say. Instead, she helped him unbutton her shirt.

"What about precautions?" Logan said softly.

She was forty-seven years old. Couldn't remember when she'd had her last period. Wasn't eager to tell this man she barely knew about her inability to have a second child.

"Not necessary," she said. "Unless . . ."

"I won't give you anything. But I'm happy to run out to a drug store. You really don't know me from Adam."

"Who had other worries," she said.

That smile.

"Here?" he said then. "Or upstairs?"

"Here," she said. "In the sunset."

When she cried out, he said he hadn't meant to hurt her.

"It's been a while," she said.

"For me, too," he said.

The next morning, awakened by a hand on her breast, she heard a whispering against the back of her neck. "How long are you staying?"

Logan, she remembered. Green bedspread. Carmel.

"My plane reservations are for Thursday. What's today?"

"Monday." His hand moved down to her hip. "Coffeemaker's broken, so I usually walk into town for breakfast. Then stop by the post office, maybe the library."

There was no mail delivery in Carmel, she remembered. The residents all had free post office boxes.

She couldn't tell if he was inviting her to have breakfast with him or politely telling her good-bye.

"I can have breakfast at my hotel."

"Alone?"

"You're welcome to come with me."

"Oh my," he said. "Double entendres before breakfast? What have I gotten myself into?"

"Me," she said, rolling toward him.

*   *   *

He took the first shower, then tickled her bare foot. "Your turn, if you'd like."

With a bar of Ivory soap, she made herself 99 and 44/100% pure, then dried off with one of the peach towels. Using an index finger, she brushed her teeth with Crest. Even tried some of his Right Guard.

No expensive toiletries for this millionaire, she noted.

Before going into town, they took Gorgeous down to the beach. Logan didn't seem to mind being seen with a woman who was not his wife.

With Gorgeous noisily enjoying her breakfast, Logan opened the front door and beckoned to Gemma to precede him. She stepped into a garden lush with trees and shrubs, followed the stone pathway to the front fence, and peered over the gate.

"Does your cottage have a name?" she asked.

"Laurel. I took the sign down. Silly to name a house, don't you think?"

She surveyed the garden. "But there's no laurel here."

He pointed to the trees on either side of the front door. "What do you think those are?"

"Not laurel," she said. "Laurel's a shrub, similar to a

rhododendron."

"These are California bay laurels," he said. "*Umbellularia californica*. You must be from out of state."

She nodded, eager to tell him, if he cared to know, that she was from Virginia.

"There's a beautiful grove of laurel in Big Sur," he said. "We could drive down there tomorrow, if you'd like."

"I would love to see Big Sur."

He closed the gate behind them and took her hand.

Outside her hotel, he asked if she'd mind having breakfast alone.

She nodded, meaning no, she didn't mind at all.

"Can you find your way back to my place? The front door's locked, but you can get in from the beach side."

"All right."

He kissed her, right there on Ocean Avenue, and walked off.

14

After changing into clean clothes, she stood in front of the mirror in her hotel room. A radiantly happy face smiled back at her.

At the front desk, there were, of course, no messages. Back in Virginia, everyone was getting along just fine without her. Had been doing so for years.

Seated at a table in the hotel restaurant, she consulted her research notes. And came up with the idea of writing a humorous article, detailing the ways in which one travel writer's pre-trip research had led her horribly astray.

She would visit the log cabin where Robinson Jeffers had begun his creative life. Describe her shock at its present condition. Wonder how he'd managed to write any poetry there at all. Admit that she'd been duped by her own romantic imagination and that, in this case anyway, the poet's writing had flourished when he was surrounded by stones.

After walking up Ocean Ave to Monte Verde Street, she turned left. Sixth Avenue, Fifth Avenue, and then Third Avenue. Hadn't the librarian said Monte Verde at Fourth? There was no Fourth. So she backtracked, concentrating on the houses this time, and there, not far from Fifth Avenue, was an old log cabin.

Dilapidated didn't begin to describe it. Still, that falling-down cabin was what had brought her to Carmel. To Logan. And to whatever might happen next.

She found a deli, bought a sandwich. To eat later. On the beach, on Logan's deck. Wherever.

Logan hadn't yet come home when she let herself in through the sliding glass door. Gorgeous was so glad to see her that Gemma couldn't help wondering. How did Logan usually spend his days?

And who was he, really? The two of them had shared their bodies but not their last names.

Once the dog had calmed down, Gemma began snooping around. No unpaid bills on the kitchen counter, or on the desk in the library/living room. Feeling only slightly guilty, she opened the desk drawers. Ballpoint pens. Paper clips. A stapler. A packet of lined notebook paper.

Logan seemed to have left his identity elsewhere.

Except for the books he'd collected. That part of him was on full display.

Next to the window beside the front door was a book with its cover facing out. *The Women at Point Sur,* by Robinson Jeffers. Below it, on a bottom shelf, were four college yearbooks.

Had Logan gone to Reed College? Since she didn't know his last name, it seemed useless to flip through pages and pages of yearbook photos, as indeed it proved to be.

Hoping to come across a bookplate on an inside cover, she began taking down some of the older books. And bingo! A full set of *The Writings of Mark Twain,* bound in red cloth, had belonged to a Logan Thomas Rhodes.

Returning to the yearbooks, she discovered that a Logan J. Rhodes had graduated from Reed College in 1960. A handsome fellow, with a familiar smile, he was from Billings, Montana. He had majored in biology and belonged to the fencing and philosophy cubs.

She ventured upstairs, where the only names hiding in the medicine cabinet in the master bath were all too familiar—Bayer, Pepto-Bismol, Desenex, BAND-AID. Not a single prescription for either Logan or his wife.

Very quietly, she opened one dresser drawer after another. Under a pile of neatly folded men's sweaters was a photo of a little girl on a beach. On the back, someone had written, "Maggie, 1975, Newport, OR."

Logan's daughter? She didn't look at all like him.

The second bedroom, stark as a prison cell, contained bunk beds with bare mattresses, a small desk and chair, and two locked file cabinets. It gave Gemma the creeps.

She was downstairs again, looking for a book Logan's wife might have inscribed to him—as a birthday present, or for Christmas—when suddenly Gorgeous lurched to her feet, her tail wagging furiously, and ran to the sliding glass door. Gemma quickly grabbed a book, any book, and opened it.

Had the universe read her mind? There, on the title page, was a note in blue ink. To Logan. With much love, Trisha.

Hurriedly, Gemma replaced the book.

"Looking for something to read?" Logan came up behind her.

Worried a guilty look might give her away, she didn't turn around. "Do you have any travel books?"

"Well, let's see." He moved toward the front door, took down a tall book from the top shelf. "Lawrence Durrell. *The Greek Islands*. Will this do?"

"Oh, yes!" she said, taking the book from him. "I've always wanted to visit Greece."

"There's a Greek restaurant on Guadalupe. We could go there for dinner."

"Great idea!"

When Logan went upstairs, Gemma set *Greece* aside and returned to the book Trisha had given him. *Slouching Towards Bethlehem* showed no signs of having ever been read.

She'd returned Joan Didion to the shelf and was reading about Corfu when Logan sank down beside her.

"This is beautifully written," she said.

"Lawrence Durrell was considered for a Nobel Prize."

"For this? I didn't know travel books were eligible."

"For *The Alexandria Quartet*, I think it was, but the Nobel folks decided his novels were too decadent."

Gemma knew nothing at all about Lawrence Durrell. "Do you like to travel?"

"Carmel is enough for me," he said.

"Tell me about Robinson Jeffers."

"He loved it here, too, or said he did. Some of his poems are pretty bleak, though."

"There's nothing I'd rather do than travel." She was ready, if he cared to know, to tell him how she'd come to Carmel on a wild goose chase.

Logan touched her cheek. "We could take a trip upstairs," he said.

"But I just arrived in Corfu." She pointed to a color photo of a large ferry. "Aren't the mountains lovely?"

"Then why don't you read to me?"

So she did.

And then they went upstairs.

The next morning, they had breakfast near Point Lobos, then followed the curving coastline south, along Highway 1. The bright blue Pacific to their right, dark green forests to their left. Rocks and boulders everywhere.

In his navy blue Jeep Cherokee, its windows down, its radio off, Logan was a very smooth shifter of gears.

"What about Gorgeous?" Gemma said. "Won't she need to go out?"

"A friend's going to stop by," Logan said.

Male or female? Gemma wondered.

They drove in silence. Waves crashed; winds blew.

"Do you like to hike?" Logan said.

"I do, yes."

"Then into the forest we'll go, to lose our minds ..."

She felt a chill. "And find our souls. John Muir, supposedly." She didn't tell him the Sierra Club couldn't confirm it. Muir *could've* said it, after all, with only the trees as witnesses.

At Pfeiffer Big Sur State Park, Gemma gathered up all the brochures and maps she could find and skimmed through them. Thinking that maybe, instead of conducting interviews with the locals, or describing a dilapidated cabin, she should stick to what she'd done in the past—compare and contrast. Hiking in Big Sur versus hiking in the Shenandoah National Park. Laurel Grove versus Hemlock Grove. Laurel (tree) versus laurel (shrub). Black-tailed deer versus white-tailed deer. Prevalence of mountain lions versus total extinction.

"The Buzzards Roost Trail is nice," Logan said.

"Are there buzzards?" She made a face.

"I've never seen one."

"You come here often, then?"

"Occasionally would be more accurate."

"With your wife?"

"I'm pretty much a loner," he said. "You're smart enough to have figured that out."

"And yet you're here with me."

He shrugged. "Go figure."

* * *

Never before had she seen such tall trees. The sky, seemingly further away than usual, was sometimes not visible at all under the lush green canopy. Occasionally she heard water rushing down to join the Big Sur River. But mostly it was quiet, an unearthly stillness.

The few hikers they encountered were friendly. But then, weren't hikers always friendly?

One couple asked where they were from. "We're visiting," Logan said without stopping to chat. "Beautiful here, isn't it?"

The redwoods were indeed giants, the oaks as well. The pine straw was a pinkish orange.

"A red carpet," she said.

"A welcome mat. You are welcome here."

"Then thank you," she said. "Thank you for bringing me."

The trail became steeper. They hiked in silence, with Logan in the lead, until he stopped and turned around. "Just a little further." He took her hand.

Suddenly, there was open sky, there was ocean.

"This is what I wanted to show you," Logan said.

Far, far below them was the Pacific, looking as calm as its name. She was too stunned to speak. The visible world consisted entirely of water and sky and forested mountains. There was nothing else, nowhere else.

Logan squeezed her hand. "Beautiful, isn't it?"

She nodded.

"Maybe buzzards used to roost up here," he said. "I'm no historian."

"It's too beautiful for buzzards," she said.

Logan stared up at the sky. "When I was a boy, I thought it would be fun to be a raptor. Spend all day, every day, soaring around on wind currents."

"That *would* be fun. I'm not sure I'd like the diet, though."

"I didn't plan to get hungry. Just float here, there, and everywhere, with not a care in the world."

They stood in silence, gazing up.

"Robinson Jeffers wrote a poem about a vulture," Logan said. "While he was lying on a hillside, resting, a vulture swooped down to see if he was dead. I think the poem ends with Jeffers wishing he had been, so that he could have experienced life after death, or heaven, or whatever."

"No!"

"I'm probably misquoting. I'll try to find the poem for you when we get back."

Again, he squeezed her hand. "Let me know when you're ready to go."

"I could stay here all day. Though I wish I had my camera."

"Photos never do this justice. Ever. Better to imprint it on your brain."

She stood there doing exactly that.

"Someone's coming, I think," Logan said. "Damn!"

Two men in lederhosen appeared.

"Guten tag," Logan said to them.

"Hello yourself," one of the men said. "Where y'all from?"

"We're floaters." Logan turned to her. "Ready to go?"

"Enjoy the view," she said to the men, then followed Logan down the trail.

Back into the woods they went. The trees, so much taller than she was used to, gave off unfamiliar scents. She couldn't remember having ever felt so happy.

"The laurel grove?" she said.

"Ah. That's on a different trail. Sorry. I'd forgotten all about that."

"No matter. I love it here."

It wasn't long before Logan left the main trail and led her along a faint path beside a stream. "Bathroom break," he said. "You stay here. I'll go down the trail a bit."

She walked into the woods and pulled some Kleenex from the packet in her jeans pocket. Then, back on the path, she kept checking her watch. It was twenty minutes before Logan appeared.

"There you are," he said. "My beautiful wood nymph."

"I was getting worried."

"Saw a rattlesnake." He was beaming. "A real beauty. Didn't want to startle it, though, so I just stood there and watched."

"Wise move. Are there copperheads here?"

"Don't think so, no."

It was another item for her compare-and-contrast list. "Plenty of copperheads where I come from."

And where is that, exactly? he could so easily have asked.

"Virginia," she said. "That's where I'm from."

"Not Tidewater. Your accent's different."

She wondered if this was progress.

"I was thinking about asking you to lie down with me on the red carpet," he said, motioning to the pine straw. "But that rattlesnake might've changed my mind."

"Snakes won't attack unless they feel threatened," she said.

"You sure about that?"

"Pretty sure. I'd be more worried about insects."

He leaned down, picked up a handful of pine needles, let them drift to the ground. "Looks fine to me."

"I don't know, Logan. Besides, it's cold up here."

"Just lie down with me. We don't have to copulate."

"But we will. We can't help ourselves. We're like addicts."

He sat down, offered her a hand, pulled her down beside him.

"I want to be on top," she said, "so the ants won't bite me."

"That can be arranged."

When they'd returned to the main trail, he put an arm around her shoulder. "I love that you were willing to do that."

She finished the thought for him. "But you don't love me."

"Please understand, Gemma. You and I, we have no future."

"Does your wife like Big Sur?" she said.

"Talking about our marriages would be completely pointless."

"So we try to enjoy the next two days, and then we never think about each other again?"

"I'll think about you. And you'll think about me. And after a while, we'll get over it."

"So are you the man in the desert?" she said a little

later. "The one signaling to the caravan that he doesn't *want* to be rescued?"

"Shelton's 'Local Knowledge.' You read that?"

"I did."

"A haunting image."

15

The next day, she returned to Carson's Café for lunch. The same waiter took her order.

"You were here a few days ago," he said. "From Virginia, right?"

She nodded.

"You look different. That Carmel glow. It's all this fresh air."

"And good coffee." She toasted him with her cup.

There were no messages for her at the hotel. She went up to her room and, after making sure she'd repacked everything, returned to the front desk and checked out. Throwing caution to the winds, where it belonged.

She trundled her roll-on suitcase down Ocean Avenue and then along Scenic Drive. At the unidentified Laurel Cottage, she opened the gate and left her suitcase by the cottage's locked front door.

There was no easy way to get to Logan's deck from the front of his house, so she went back the way she'd come, taking the first set of public steps down to the beach. People smiled at her, as if she were one of their neighbors. Friendly dogs came up to her. She felt completely at home.

That night, they had dinner at a restaurant perched on a rocky cliff above the ocean. Her suggestion. She'd noticed the restaurant on the drive down to Big Sur and thought maybe she could include it in the article she was thinking about trying to write. If she still knew how to write. If she could stand to leave out the most important details. To remember not to remember.

After dinner, they went outside. The sun was setting, the ocean spraying the rocks far below.

Gemma put her arms around Logan and kissed him. "I could change my plane reservations," she said. "Stay a little longer."

"Yes, that occurred to me."

"Well, then?" She was afraid she'd never be able to keep such an enormous secret. From her husband, her daughter, her parents. Surely, they'd know the minute they saw her. It would be written all over her face.

He shook his head. "The longer we wait to say good-bye, the harder it will be."

"If I wrote to you, at Laurel Cottage, Carmel," she said, "would you get the letter?"

"Good question."

"Or you could write to me." She took out her wallet, extracted one of her business cards. "Gemma Sommerset was my maiden name. Back home, I'm Gemma McKenna."

He examined the card. "A travel writer. You never said."

"And you never said what you do."

"Not a lot, these days. Read. Think. Walk the dog."

She gave up.

Later, on his deck, she asked if it was allowed on the beach.

"Is what allowed?"

"You know. Sex. Under a full moon." She pointed to the sky.

"No idea. I'm sure it happens. My steps are private property. We could try it there."

She shook her head. "Splinters."

He threw back his head, roared with laughter. "Gemma, I'd vowed not to say this, but I'm going to miss you."

"If we did it in the woods, then we can surely manage on a beach."

"I don't want to get arrested. And neither do you."

"We can wear trench coats. That way no one will know what we're up to."

He went inside and returned with two trench coats. "Khaki or green?"

"Which one's lined?"

"They both are. It can get chilly here at night."

She chose the green one and began removing her clothes. "If the police show up, then we can just get to our feet and walk off."

"Sounds like you've had a lot of practice."

"I'd never even had sex in the woods. You're a bad influence on me."

But she was forgetting. Sex in the woods, no. In the clover, yes.

Down the steps to the beach they went, naked under their trench coats. Beyond the moon, the sky was fuzzy with stars.

"There's no one here." She took his hand, led him to the ocean's edge, where the waves were gentle and rhythmic. "Not a soul in sight."

"Name all the beaches you've had sex on," he said.

"This will be the first one."

He scanned the beach, north to south, then let go of her hand and walked backwards. Sat down on the softer sand and unbuttoned his coat.

"You're flashing me?"

He lay back. "I'm asking you to get on top again. I want to see stars."

"You keep your eyes *open*?"

"The better to see you with, my dear."

They didn't get arrested. Not there, on the open beach, or later, in the softer sand at the bottom of Logan's steps.

"Let's sleep here tonight," she said. They were curled together, keeping each other warm. "It's so comfortable."

"I'd really prefer a bed."

"May I tell you something?"

"Oh, please don't."

"I'm from Virginia, as you know. I grew up in Lynchburg and now live in Lexington. My daughter's finishing her sophomore year at the University of Virginia. Her name is Noreen."

No reply.

"Where are you from?" Gemma went on. "If you don't mind my asking."

"No place in particular. I've lived all over."

"'Billings, Montana,'" she recited. "'Biology major. Fencing team. Philosophy club.'"

He straightened his legs, pushed her away. "You've

been *spying* on me?"

"Why all the secrecy?" There were so many questions. Was his wife really in San Francisco? Did he love her? Did they have a little girl named Maggie?

"I'm an ordinary man with an ordinary life."

"Bullshit." Gemma sat up, pulled the trench coat tight. "We're in love, you and I, and our spouses have no idea."

"You'd be surprised, Gemma, how extremely ordinary that is."

"This has happened to you before?"

"Never. And I'll never let it happen again. It's far too painful."

She was close to tears. "I want to see you again."

"Oh, Gemma. As my mother used to say, be grateful for what you have." He pulled her back down in the sand and nestled up behind her. "I've already told you. We have no future. Remember my saying that?"

Of course she did.

"What we have is this." He slipped his hand inside her trench coat. "This magic. If you can be patient with me. It's been a long night."

"Logan," she said. "I'm not insatiable."

"So you're satiable?"

"Let's just lie here." In the soft sand, on the empty beach, under the wide-eyed moon. "A little longer. Do you mind?"

But Logan had fallen asleep.

The next morning, on the sidewalk outside the airport, Logan kissed her goodbye. "Let's be brave about this," he said. "We stole a few days from eternity."

Whatever that meant.

She thanked him for a lovely time.

He wished her a safe trip.

Then Logan Rhodes, mystery man, got back in his Jeep and drove off.

16

On a warm Sunday afternoon in September, Gemma and Tim were returning to Lexington from Charlottesville, where Noreen had begun her junior year at UVA. During lunch, Noreen had talked on and on about her new boyfriend. Marshall Something.

Unlike Gemma, Noreen had not been sent to college to find a husband. If that happened, fine, but a degree was equally important. Having become interested in environmental issues, Noreen had spent the summer after her freshman year working for a nonprofit in DC. Gemma had driven her daughter to Washington, helped her find a small apartment, and covered the first month's rent.

Now, with the car's air conditioning going full blast, Gemma sat staring out the passenger-side window, her mind completely blank—a skill she'd perfected over the summer. Eyes wide open, not seeing a thing. Ears only vaguely aware that Tim was, as usual, singing along with his favorite radio station.

When he suddenly fell silent, she glanced over. Saw

the tense look on Tim's face, his tight grip on the steering wheel.

The Eagles kept right on singing.

And Gemma knew. To Tim, *she* was the wife in the Eagles song. The one who couldn't hide her lyin' eyes.

Without looking at her, Tim flicked the radio off. In the terrible silence, which lasted the rest of the way home, another truth surfaced. Gemma wasn't the only one. Tim had been there, too. "The cheatin' side of town."

Seconds after he'd turned into their driveway, Tim was out of the car. He slammed the door, and, without a word, took off.

The astute accountant had put two and two together. More than four months pregnant, Gemma was beginning to show.

She was at the stove, mashing potatoes with a vengeance, when she heard the front door close. Tim clomped down the hall and into the kitchen.

He came up behind her, reached around, and gently touched her tummy. "When were you going to tell me?" he said, his voice hoarse.

"When did you notice?" she said.

"Gemma! I'm not blind. I thought it was just middle-age spread."

She'd been both dreading this conversation and looking forward to it. Surprise, surprise! Looked like she *could* get pregnant after all, despite what Dr. Mayhew, Tim's longtime golf buddy and her ob-gyn, had said years ago. She'd hoped that what seemed to her like a miracle would somehow put the right words in her mouth. Instead, her mind was completely blank.

Tim stepped away, opened the silverware drawer. "I blamed *you.* All these years, I thought it was your fault."

Gemma added butter to the potatoes, a little salt. "Maybe we were just unlucky."

"Looks like *you* got lucky. In California?"

"Yeah."

"Does he know?" Tim said.

"No."

"You gonna tell him?"

Gemma hadn't quite decided. "No."

"I almost didn't come back just now. Thought about getting a motel room, and maybe that's exactly what I should do. Never been so angry in my entire life."

"At the doctors?"

"You *cheated* on me, Gemma. You're my *wife.* Do we need steak knives?"

"Not unless you're planning to stab me."

The table in their kitchen was oak, not redwood. Tim began setting it.

"Husbands aren't supposed to cheat, either." She realized that her 'little trips,' as Tim referred to them, had given him ample opportunity. "I should be just as angry at you."

He didn't deny it. He didn't say anything at all.

She opened the oven, where leftover pork chops and cornbread muffins were warming. "Want a salad?" she said.

"What the hell kind of salad?"

"I'll take that as a 'no thanks.'" She served two plates, set the plates on the table, and sat down.

Tim filled two water glasses, which spilled over when he plunked them down on the table. Once seated, he stared at his plate. "I'm not hungry."

"Well, I am." Gemma picked up a fork.

"I guess so. Eating for two."

"You might feel a little better after you've had a few bites."

Tim drank his water instead. The entire glass. When it was empty, he stood up, opened a cabinet, and filled the glass half full of bourbon.

"We need to think this through," he said when he was seated again.

Gemma waited.

Tim poked at a pork chop with his fork. "I always wanted more children."

"So did I. You know that."

"I just don't want someone else's kid."

"OK. I can understand that."

"I mean." Tim cut up a pork chop, ate half of it. As if he were hungry. "It's not like adopting."

"OK, Tim. Do you want me to move out?"

For months now—when she'd thought about it, which she'd tried not to—Gemma had wondered what she'd do, where she'd go, when this day arrived. Move in with her parents? Tell them lies? What lies?

"Who was she?" Gemma suddenly wanted to know. "Someone I know?"

"There was more than one, Gemma."

"Here in Lexington?"

"Natural Bridge, the first time. Terrible mistake."

"While I was out of town?"

"Does it matter?"

No, she realized, there were more important concerns. "I don't know how to tell my parents."

"Now that's just plain silly. You're a married woman. No problem there."

So he was willing for her parents to think it was *his* child?

"Just wear a maternity dress next time you see

them. Act happy."

"That's the strangest thing," Gemma said. "I *am* happy."

"Well, all right. Guess that's a good thing." He got up from the table, left the kitchen, circled around through the dining room and living room.

"I'm not *happy*," he said when he returned. "I mean, this hurts, Gemma. It really does. Even though I deserve it. Tit for tat, an eye for an eye, it all evens out in the end."

Tim's Platitudes. The book for which Gemma had been saving up material for decades.

"Are you in love with him?" he said.

Madly, she thinks while replying, "It was only a few days, Tim. You haven't touched me in years."

"I know, I know. What does he do for a living?"

"I have no idea."

"Where'd you meet him?"

"On the beach."

"Yeah, I know the type. Beach bum. Surfer dude. What kind of car does he drive?"

"Jeep Cherokee." *With its own cute little garage beside the garden in front of a very expensive cottage.*

"Red, I'll bet."

"Dark blue. Is there any wine?"

"You're not having wine. You know better than that.

No more liquor, of any sort, until, what, February?"

She wondered why her unfaithful husband was acting so protective of a tiny fetus he'd had no part in creating. Then she remembered his high school girlfriend, the reason he hadn't wanted to have sex before marriage. Tim had wanted that baby, too.

Was that it? She decided not to ask.

"Did I tell you? I'm trying to write about Big Sur, instead of Carmel. Not making much progress, though." Every time she sat down at her desk, the rush of memories prevented her from coming up with more than a sentence or two.

"Is that where you stayed, Big Sur, after you left the hotel in Carmel? I'm going to need the receipt, come tax time."

"I'll look for it."

"Or duh," he said as he smacked his forehead. "Maybe you stayed with him at his place?"

"Big Sur Lodge," Gemma said. "By myself. I must have a receipt for the rental car, too." How easy it was to lie, once you'd begun.

"You're actually pregnant." Tim shook his head. "Mayhew hasn't said a word to me."

"He doesn't know," Gemma said. "I haven't seen a doctor yet."

His eyes went wide. "Don't you think it's time?"

"I'll find another doctor, someone you don't play golf with."

Tim nodded. "Might be better. Under the circumstances."

"Someone whose advice I can trust."

Again, he nodded. Said he guessed doctors sometimes made mistakes, just like accountants.

"I'm as surprised by this as you are," she said.

"Beach bum couldn't afford a condom?" Tim said. "Never mind. Spare me the details."

She thought back to the full moon, that night on the beach. The lush forests in Big Sur. Perhaps modern medicine didn't give Mother Nature the credit she deserved.

Again, Tim got to his feet, took a slow lap around their house. Jointly owned. The mortgage almost paid off.

"What should we tell Noreen?" he said when he returned. "When should we tell her?"

"She'll be home for Thanksgiving."

"By then, you won't have to say a word. She'll take one look at you and go, 'Mom!'"

Gemma couldn't help smiling. "So you're not going to kick me out? At least not right away?"

"What would you do if I did?"

"Find somewhere in the mountains to camp out."

"Until February?"

"I'd rather stay here, if that's all right. At least until the baby's born."

Tim nodded, as if he agreed.

"Let's wait to tell people," Gemma said. "Here in Lexington, it will become obvious. And if I miscarry—a real possibility at my age—that will be obvious, too."

"What about telling my mother?"

After the HUD-authorized repairs were finally completed, Granny Noreen had refused to return to Buena Vista. Said the flood had been a message from God, telling her she belonged in Florida with her daughter.

Realizing there was no use arguing, Tim had sold the house where he'd grown up and then sent his mother the money. Agreed that they would visit each other from time to time.

When little Noreen was five, Tim and Gemma had taken her to Tallahassee at Christmastime. Twelve hours, each way, in the car, which Tim refused ever to do again. Instead, Noreen began flying to Florida alone, spending several weeks each summer at what she and her grandmother called Cooking Camp.

Gemma had returned from North Carolina knowing how to ride a horse, do a jackknife off the diving board, and aim an arrow at a colorful round target. Noreen returned from Florida knowing how to make chicken tetrazzini, shrimp scampi, braised pork chops with apples, etc., etc.

"Let's call Tallahassee on Thanksgiving," Gemma said. "Break the news while your mother's basting the turkey."

"Then, to be fair, we can't tell your parents right away, either."

"Fine with me," Gemma said.

Tim went to the stove, served himself seconds. Poured himself more bourbon. Sat back down.

"I've been thinking," he said. "The tax laws are kinder to married couples."

Which might make divorce especially hard on a millionaire. "Then we both stay here?" she said. "See how things go?"

He raised his empty glass to her. "Why not? We're old hands at that."

17

For years—nearly every morning, unless it was pouring rain—Gemma had climbed the steps up to the deck in the dark. Seated in a dark-green lounge chair, drinking coffee from the same old thermos, she'd allowed the colors of a brand-new day to work their magic.

Having returned from Carmel in a dreary funk, she'd welcomed the familiar routine. But once Tim knew she was pregnant, he insisted the steps were an accident waiting to happen. Never mind that she shouldn't be drinking coffee—not on the deck, not anywhere. No alcohol, no caffeine, until after the baby was born.

Instead of reminding him that she'd been climbing those steps, in the dark, for years, she went back to greeting the sun from the window in Noreen's room. Began sleeping in there, too.

But then, on a crisp morning in October, Tim had to leave, very early, for a meeting in Roanoke. As excited as a child, Gemma filled her old thermos with coffee and, very slowly, climbed the steps to the deck in the dark.

Exhilarated—feeling like her old self—she sat down in her chair. Over her nightgown she was wearing a raincoat, an old London Fog, with a zip-out lining that had to be dry cleaned. Smaller than the coat she'd worn that last night on the beach in Carmel but otherwise identical.

She could remember everything she and Logan had said to each other. Wished there was a way she could tell him: *Guess what? If all goes well, you'll be a father soon.*

Would he smile that smile of his?

Except for a few pecks on the cheek, Tim hadn't touched her at all, for which she was extremely grateful.

"It's OK to have sex with your husband," Dr. Singh, her new ob-gyn, had said. Dr. Singh had four children of her own. "Eat whatever you want. Avoid alcohol. Relax. Don't worry. You're in excellent health." She'd smiled, then added, "And so very lucky."

But Gemma did worry. At her age, so many things could go wrong, for both her and the baby. Miscarriages were common. She didn't want to know whether it was a boy or a girl and was even worried that someone might slip up and tell her.

As the sky began to lighten, revealing clouds tinted

with peach and orange, she set the thermos down and went to the railing. Wasn't Gemma Sommerset McKenna one of the luckiest people on earth? Forty-seven years old, with a baby on the way. A husband who seemed at least okay with the idea that the baby was not, biologically, his.

Instead of waiting for Thanksgiving, she'd told her daughter on the phone. Asked Noreen to keep the news a secret for now.

"Un-be-*lieve*-able!" had been the astute response. Noreen had sounded excited, claimed she couldn't wait for Thanksgiving, insisted she would do all the turkey-lifting—Gemma was not even to try.

While absorbing the radiant dawn, Gemma became aware of movement down below: a doe, rustling through the fallen leaves, with a buck in careful pursuit. It soon became clear that the doe was leading the buck on, allowing him to get his hopes up.

"Go for it," Gemma whispered to them, and after a lot of prancing around, they did.

All creatures had sex, one way or another. The birds, the bees, even elephants and polar bears. Only humans told their children it was wrong, tried to set rules for when and where. What a shock, then, to realize that even preachers do it. Teachers do it.

Your own parents . . . .

18

The house in Lynchburg, an English Tudor, had always been popular with trick-or-treaters. Above the lower floor's dark bricks, wooden timbers framed rectangles of creamy stucco—a fairy-tale house during the day, a witches' abode at night. The Halloween sun was setting as Tim parked on the side street.

"I'm a little worried about this," he said. "Are you?"

"Let's hope," Gemma said, "they'll rise to the occasion."

He took her arm, and they followed the flagstone walkway around to the front of the house. Maryl, wearing an orange sweater and black slacks, was waiting for them on the front doorstep.

"Saw you drive up," she said, grinning like a child. "Like my costume?"

"What, no mask?" Gemma gave her mother a hug.

"The better to see you with, my dear. It's been ages! Come on in."

On the hall table sat a large basket containing candy bars and packets of corn candy. Ever the Southern gentleman, Carson gave Gemma a kiss on the cheek and shook Tim's hand. He then took their coats and hung them in the hall closet.

"I remember that smock," Maryl said. "Or would it be called a tunic these days?" She frowned at Gemma. "Don't I?"

Gemma nodded. She'd discovered her old maternity clothes in a box in the basement. "You know how I can't throw anything away."

"So this is a Halloween costume?"

Gemma tried to smile. "Not a scary one, I hope." She took a breath, gathered her courage, said the words. "I'm pregnant."

Still frowning, Maryl shook her head.

"What wonderful news!" Carson said.

"This is a trick, right?" Maryl said. "And you're expecting some candy in return?"

Tim spoke up. "We were as surprised as you are."

Gemma gave him a grateful smile.

"I need to sit down," Maryl said, and she did so, on the stairs. "How long have you been keeping this a secret from your very own mother? Five or six months, looks like."

"I didn't want you to be sad if, you know, something happened."

Maryl seemed to be considering this. "So, in July, when we all went to the fireworks, you were . . . expecting?"

Gemma thought back. "I didn't even know it myself then."

"A grandfather again, at my age!" Carson, smiling, pointed to his white hair.

Maryl, also white-haired, simply said, "When?"

"The doctor thinks it'll be sometime in February," Gemma said.

"Dr. Mayhew?"

"No, I'm going to Dr. Singh," Gemma said.

"Sing a song? Who's he?"

"A woman. Her husband teaches chemistry at VMI."

"This may be too much for your mother to take in right now," Carson said.

As if on cue, the doorbell rang. Tim opened the door, and there, on the flagstones, was a boy on a bicycle. A "creature" wrapped in a towel sat in the basket. "It's Elliott and E.T.," Tim called out. "Our very first trick-or-treaters." He asked if they'd prefer a Hershey bar or corn candy.

"Both," the boy said. "Some for him and some for me."

Tim stepped outside and dropped the candy into Elliott's paper bag. "Fly away now," he said, and they rode off.

"Didn't even say thank you," Maryl said. "No manners these days."

"I think I need a drink," Carson said. "Tim, will you join me?"

"Maybe one," Tim said. "I'm driving."

"I can drive back," Gemma said. "I still fit behind the steering wheel."

"I'll have a drink," Maryl said. "A stiff one."

While Tim and her father dealt with the trick-or-treaters, Gemma sat obediently with her mother on the loveseat in the den. Emanating from the kitchen across the hall were the distinctive odors of Brunswick stew, the Colonial Virginia recipe handed down and adapted by generations of Sommersets. The Colonists had stewed rabbit or squirrel—or even venison—but Maryl used chicken.

"I'm still trying to take this in," she said, staring into a glass of bourbon.

"So am I," Gemma said. "It was a shock to me, too."

"Are you healthy?"

"Dr. Singh says so."

"But you seem so thin. Are you eating enough?"

"Thin? Where?"

Maryl stared at her. "Your face looks different. Your neck."

"Gee, thanks."

"I think you should move in with us, when the time comes." Maryl sipped her bourbon. "The hospital here is better than yours, and it's only minutes away. I could have you there in no time."

"I'd very much like it if you would stop worrying." Gemma tasted her orange juice, took a few Wheat Thins from the bowl on the coffee table. Nat's favorite snack.

"But you're forty-seven years old."

"Old enough to choose my own hospital," Gemma pointed out.

Maryl sighed. "Why did you wait so long to tell me? I get that it's a risky pregnancy. But I'm your mother. The only mother you'll ever have."

"Then do me a favor. Be happy for me."

"Honey, I am happy."

Gemma had a sudden urge to tell her mother everything. No one knew the entire story, not even Tim. As the fetus grew, so did the strain of keeping such an enormous secret. She'd even considered telling Dr. Singh but decided against it.

"You want to know what's going on in your children's lives," Maryl said. "You hope they'll keep on needing you, asking for your advice. What happens instead is that they grow up and reject you."

"If I were rejecting you, then we wouldn't even be here tonight." Gemma set the sour-tasting orange juice down.

"Have you thought about a name?"

"Laurel," Gemma said.

"And if it's a boy?"

"Laurel."

"But he'd get teased at school."

"Exactly what Tim said. Laurel's a boy's name, too."

"Why Laurel?"

Gemma said the same thing that had silenced Tim. "Would you prefer Rhododendron?"

"What about Nathanial?"

She'd considered this but then realized that having a little boy named Nat around, who might look like Logan, would be unbearable. The two humans she'd loved the most but would never see again.

"Please, let's not argue." She glanced up at the wall above the TV, expecting to see her father's old hunting trophy, a buck with an impressive rack of antlers. Instead, there were two framed photos. Sommerset men in their Army uniforms, the son the spitting image of his dad.

"What happened to the deer?" Gemma said.

"Mold. Your father sprayed it with something, and wiped it down, but the mold kept coming back."

"So where is it now?"

"He put it in a huge leaf bag and set it out for the garbage. I think he might have said a prayer over it."

Gemma was glad for an excuse to smile. "Did we ever eat venison?"

Maryl shook her head. "The only butcher who did that sort of thing charged an arm and a leg. Your father's little joke. Remember Mamie, who plucked and cleaned the doves he shot? She passed away last summer."

"What pleasure did he get from killing innocent animals? I never understood that."

"It's how he was brought up. Men went hunting together. It was part of the culture here. Still is."

Like fighting in wars, Gemma managed not to say. "Did your father have guns?"

"Oh, honey. Think about it. Wild animals live free, with very little risk of being shot. The meat we buy in grocery stores? Those animals were doomed from the very beginning. I'd rather be killed in the wild than commercially slaughtered. Wouldn't you?"

"Never thought of it that way."

Gemma had been in high school when her father gave up hunting for good. He'd mistakenly shot a doe, who was still alive when he found her, so he'd had to shoot her again, with those big brown eyes staring up at him.

Hardest thing he'd ever done in his life, or so he'd said at the time.

So why had he continued to keep his trophy buck on display in the den?

Gemma stared at the two photos taking the dead deer's place. Her father, who had enlisted to support his country, and her brother, who'd let himself be drafted so as not to disappoint his father.

"Our lives have patterns." Maryl swallowed the last of her bourbon. "Sometimes it feels like someone else is doing the weaving, and you're not supposed to notice, but then you see what's taking shape, or think you do." She paused. "And what you see is who you are."

"Not sure I follow."

"The choices we make."

"Or don't make."

"Not choosing counts as a choice," said the statistician. "Life's a total crapshoot, just one roll of the dice after another. Sometimes, we get lucky and beat the odds." She raised her empty glass. "So, congratulations, honey. I'm happy for you. Truly I am."

Gemma nodded.

"Do me a favor?"

"Sure." Gemma said this warily, afraid of where her mother's thoughts were headed.

"Go stir the Brunswick stew? Make sure it's not sticking to the bottom of the pan."

Grateful for an excuse to leave the room, Gemma hurried into the kitchen. She removed the lid from the stainless-steel pot, found a long-handled spoon, and stirred. Her Sommerset ancestors had surely done the very same thing, with a similar stew, in a different sort of pot. Cast iron, maybe. She wondered if this was the sort of pattern her mother was rambling on about.

Maryl had spent her entire married life taking care of her family. Being faithful to her husband, Gemma was certain of this. Managing alone, while he was in Europe and then in Japan, and later, moving with him and their two young children to his hometown, where she knew no one at all. Cooking his meals. Cleaning his house. Ironing his shirts.

Plopping his little dead doves into boiling water.

Not blaming him for their beloved son's death.

"Stew's been stirred," Gemma reported from the den's doorway.

"Thank you." Maryl patted the loveseat, inviting Gemma to sit. "When will we get to see your article about Carmel?"

Gemma remained standing. "I ran into some problems, due to sloppy research before I got there."

"Uh oh. So you're still writing it?"

"Thinking about it," Gemma lied.

"You were there when? In May?"

Gemma nodded. She could hear her mother's mental calculator predicting the possibilities. Carmel five months ago. Baby due in four.

"Tim seems pleased." Again, Maryl patted the loveseat. "About the baby."

"He is, yes." Gemma leaned against the door jamb. "He'd always hoped for another child."

"Will you at least think about having the baby here in Lynchburg?"

"What I think," Gemma said, "is that the choice of hospital is up to my doctor. I'll mention it to her, OK?"

"So hard to predict, pregnancy. So many different variables and possible outcomes." Maryl sighed. "Still, I got pregnant with you the first time I tried. Talk about pure luck!"

All Gemma had ever been told about sex was not to have it until she was married. Never before had her mother even hinted at the sexual act itself.

"With Nat," Maryl went on, "it was different. Your father felt so very lucky to have made it home from Europe. He was on cloud nine. And then the Army told him they were sending him off to Japan." She studied her empty glass. "He didn't want to go, didn't think he should have to."

"But he was a good soldier," Gemma said quickly.

"The best." Maryl seemed fixated on her empty glass. "Your children are everything, you know. Everything."

A silence bloomed.

Again, Maryl patted the loveseat. "Come tell me about Carmel."

Reluctantly, Gemma sat down. Took a deep breath. Described her visit to Carmel's library, where she'd learned that the log cabin she'd come to see was in shambles. She then told her mother about locating the cabin, to verify that it was in fact falling apart, and then trying to come up with something else to write about.

"Like what?"

"Like all those millionaires in Carmel with their very small, very expensive houses."

"Did you meet any of them?"

"Some of them come to the library in the morning, and sit in front of the fireplace, reading the newspaper. A wood-burning fireplace in the public library—that's Carmel for you."

"Did you interview any of them?"

"I never worked up the nerve," Gemma said. "Instead, I wandered around that picturesque little town like someone on vacation. It's been so long since I've had a real vacation. I miss our trips to Myrtle Beach."

She told her mother about the multiple flights of steps leading down to Carmel Beach. About wading into the surprisingly cold Pacific Ocean.

The millionaire with the Dalmatian, the man who'd guarded her shoes and socks? The way he'd smiled when she realized why no one else was in the icy-cold water?

Logan's smile. She wanted so very badly to tell someone, even her mother, about that smile.

That she was the only one who knew the whole story had only added to the stress. Despite his kindness and generosity, she'd lied to Tim. Not telling Logan, who'd sent her packing, was a different sort of lie.

Fontana had always been so very good at keeping secrets. But was a total failure at keeping in touch.

"Did you take long walks on the beach?" her mother said. "At Myrtle Beach, you'd sometimes be gone for so long that I'd worry you wouldn't be able to find your way back to us. But somehow you always did."

I got pregnant on the beach, in the moonlight, Gemma suddenly wanted to tell her mother. Either there or under the redwoods in Big Sur.

But Tim saved her. "You gotta see this," he said from the doorway. "Both of you. Come quickly."

In the front hallway stood two trick-or-treaters. The taller one, in an ankle-length, strapless dress, exuded the serene beauty of a Homecoming Queen. The younger girl was wrapped in plastic sheeting, her face gray, her lips white.

"I don't understand," Maryl said.

"Laura Palmer," Gemma said. "From *Twin Peaks*."

"I had to stop watching." Maryl said. "That show gave me nightmares."

"Wasn't that the whole point?" Carson held out the basket of candy to the girls. "You two win first prize. Take all you want."

The Homecoming Queen filled her treat bag. "None for her. She's dead."

"But that's not fair," Carson said.

The girl shrugged a bare shoulder. "Life's not fair."

On their drive back to Lexington, Tim kept taking deep breaths, letting them out.

"What is it?" Gemma said. "What's wrong?"

"I didn't like having to lie to your father," Tim said.

"What did you tell him?"

"Nothing. I let him believe I'm the father of your child."

"Isn't that what we agreed to?"

"It is," Tim said. "Did you tell your mother the truth?"

"Of course not."

He turned on the radio. Willie Nelson, as if on cue, was excusing his extramarital affairs by insisting to his wife that she was always on his mind.

"Is he on *your* mind?" Tim said.

"Who?" Gemma said.

"Who do you think? 'Surfer dude'."

"Tim. You've never been to a beach, never seen a surfboard. How do you even know that term?"

"Maybe I'm a little smarter than you think," Tim said. "So. Do you? Think about him?"

"Not really." A flat-out lie. She thought about Logan all day long and half the night. Wondered where he was, what he was doing. If he was with his wife.

"So," Tim said. "We lied to your parents tonight, both of us. And you've already lied to our daughter, all by yourself. That leaves my mother and my sister still to go."

"We've told people I'm pregnant. Which is completely true. Also true: you and I are married. No one's going to ask who the father is."

Tim said nothing.

"'Oh, what a tangled web we weave, when first we practice to deceive.'"

"Shakespeare?" Tim asked.

"Sir Walter Scott," Gemma said. "'Practiced in the art of deception.' That'll be us in a few years. Who said that?"

"Mick Jagger. Keith Richards."

"Of course. I knew that."

"My favorite poets," Tim said, "all play guitar."

<h1 style="text-align:center">19</h1>

As it turned out, Laurel McKenna was born in Charlottesville, a few minutes after midnight, on Sunday, January 20, 1991. One of the very last Capricorn babies of the year, she weighed in at just four and a half pounds.

At lunch that day, before Laurel's arrival, Noreen had asked her parents if they'd like to see Monticello, where plans were underway to admit the truth: Thomas Jefferson had owned slaves. One of her history professors was involved in researching what future visitors would be told, and she was curious to know what the current tour was like.

"But only if you feel up to it, Mom," she said.

"Sure," Gemma said. "I haven't been to Monticello since I was in high school."

"Did you see where the slaves lived?" Noreen said.

"Don't think so." What Gemma remembered was Jefferson's library. And how small his bed was.

"You didn't," Noreen said. "Slavery wasn't even mentioned. But that'll change soon."

Once they'd arrived at Monticello, Gemma needed help getting out of the car.

"What's wrong?" Tim said, once she was standing.

"My back hurts, that's all. That chair I sat in at lunch had slats in all the wrong places."

"You're not in labor, are you?" he said.

"Of course not. It's too early for that."

"The hospital here is very good," Noreen said. "I even know where it is."

"Don't need a hospital," Gemma insisted. "Just need some-where comfortable to sit for a while. Or maybe lie down."

She closed the car's front door, opened a back one, and climbed in. Remembering what labor had felt like with Noreen, she felt certain this was different. This was nothing.

"You two go ahead," she said. "I'll be fine here."

Tim and Noreen must have exchanged father-daughter glances, as they often did, and come to the same conclusion. Soon, they were on their way back to Charlottesville.

Gemma lay down on the seat, closed her eyes.

"Emergency!" she heard Tim shout.

"Don't we want Maternity?" Noreen said.

"Emergency will know where to send her," Tim said. He stopped the car, opened the back door, and helped Gemma out. Noreen then took his place behind the wheel and drove off to find somewhere to park.

They'd always been a good team, Tim and Noreen.

"For the umpteenth time, I'm not in labor," Gemma insisted. "This will end up costing us a lot of money for nothing."

Without a word, Tim took her arm, guided her safely through the heavy glass door.

What Gemma would remember from those five days in the hospital was a chorus of voices:

A nurse in the delivery room: *Your baby came so fast!*

Tim, changing the words to a Kris Kristofferson song: *Laurel is a Capricorn, she'll eat organic food.*

Carson, bowing to Gemma: *Well done, Okasama.*

Maryl, with a worried frown: *But she weighs less than a bag of sugar.*

Noreen, grinning: *My tiny little born-in-Charlottesville sis.*

The other Noreen, along with Tim's sister, Dory, arrived from Florida a few weeks later. Having made their way up the stairs to what Tim and Gemma were once again calling "the nursery," they peered into the new crib, where little Laurel was sleeping.

Gemma touched her daughter's cheek. "You have visitors," she whispered, and Laurel opened her eyes.

"Good Lord!" Granny Noreen said. "That baby looks exactly like my Great Aunt Clara!"

"Congratulations to us," Tim whispered to Gemma that night. "Seems like we've fooled everyone."

20

The ruined Raggedy Ann and Andy curtains had been replaced with material similar to the official McKenna Scottish plaid. Noreen had enjoyed the ritual of closing the curtains at night. Eager for sunrise, Gemma left them open.

It was hardly a surprise that Laurel's first word was "sun." She was sitting up in the crib when she said it.

"Sun, yes!" Gemma said. "Hooray for Laurel!"

"Sun." Laurel said it again, with a tiny fist pump. And an oh-so-familiar smile.

A short walk from their house—up the hill and across Main Street—the Stonewall Jackson Cemetery contained tombstones dating back to the 1700s. In its center, an enormous statue of Jackson called attention to the large, circular area where he and his relatives were buried.

In other sections of the cemetery, smaller family plots were surrounded by ornate, wrought iron fences. This was the area Laurel loved to visit.

Having steered the stroller off a main pathway, Gemma would lift Laurel out and set her down in the grass. One day, after crawling through dead leaves, Laurel grabbed onto an iron fence post and tried to pull herself up.

"Let me help," Gemma said.

An eternal prison for those buried inside the enclosure, the ancient wrought iron railing allowed Laurel McKenna, for the first time, to stand on her own.

A week or so later, Laurel took her first steps.

"You taught her to walk in the cemetery?" Tim was not pleased.

"She already knew what to do," Gemma said. "All I did was watch."

It was on one of these trips to the cemetery that a small tombstone caught Gemma's eye. The solitary grave was not far from the stone wall separating the cemetery from Main Street.

The simple inscription (GSM, d. 1792) gave Gemma Sommerset McKenna chills. Who was this person? A woman, surely. Remembered by a man who'd never bothered to ask how old she was? Who perhaps had a wife and child of his own but felt compelled to do the right thing with her remains?

At three years old, glancing neither to the right nor the left as she strode down the aisle, Laurel was the flower girl at her sister Noreen's wedding in Lexington. By the end of the ceremony, Laurel had gained a brother-in law, Marshall Shepherd.

A year later, in a hospital in Fairfax, Virginia, Laurel met her newborn niece, Felicia Shepherd, Gemma and Tim's first grandchild.

"I smiled at her," Laurel said excitedly, "and she smiled back."

"Everyone smiles when you do,"Tim said. "It's some sort of magic."

While listening to a Dixie Chicks CD in the kitchen one afternoon, Gemma realized that Laurel was singing along.

"'Wide Open Spaces,'" Laurel wailed. Echoing Natalie Maines' longing for new beginnings, the freedom to make "big mistakes."

"You're the best thing that ever happened to me," Gemma said when the song had ended.

"Loving Arms" was next. Laurel kept right on singing.

"How did you learn all the words?" Gemma asked.

"Mom," Laurel said. "You play these songs all the

time."

"Do I?"

"You know you do. And then Daddy comes home, and you turn the Dixie Chicks off."

"Because it's time for dinner."

"Mary Lou's parents listen to Mozart during dinner."

"They don't talk to each other?"

Laurel shook her head.

"Well, dinner's a good time for family conversation," Gemma said. "Don't you think?"

Laurel shrugged her shoulders. "Daddy might like to listen to Willie Nelson."

"He'd rather listen to you."

"I know." And Laurel smiled.

The familiar smile that took Gemma's breath away.

Part III

Death and Remembrance

21

In January of 1971, a year after Nat was reported missing, Gemma and Tim had attended a memorial service for him in the same church in Lynchburg where they'd been married.

Knowing that long-lost soldiers sometimes returned home, in real life as well as in fiction, Gemma had worried that such a formal and very public goodbye might jinx things for her beloved brother. She'd considered using seven-month-old Noreen as an excuse to stay home.

But something else had been clear to her as well. This particular missing soldier, wherever he might be, would want his sister to go to the service, if only for their parents' sake.

Not long after the minister had begun talking about Nat, Noreen, with perfect timing, became fussy. Having managed to escape quietly, down a side aisle, with her baby in her arms, Gemma, her heels clicking on the stone floor of the church vestibule, began pacing slowly back and forth. Even with Noreen finally asleep, she'd kept walking. All the while whispering to Nat: *This is your niece. Her name is Noreen. Please, please, please come home.*

A month later, she'd managed not to participate in the small ceremony beside the new tombstone in the cemetery where Nat was not buried. It took decades for her to be able to accept the truth. She would never, ever see her brother again.

On the morning of April 10, 1996, which would have been Nat's fiftieth birthday, Gemma dropped Laurel off at kindergarten and headed for Lynchburg, wondering if maybe the time had finally come to try to tell her brother good-bye. If so, then she'd try to do it all by herself, and in her own way.

Laurel, at five, already knew about her Uncle Nat, having pointed to his photo one day and asked who he was. The male relative she was not yet aware of was her biological father. She would be told, Tim and Gemma agreed. When she turned twelve? Sixteen? They hadn't yet decided.

One thing Gemma *had* decided was that Laurel (and Tim) would then be told the truth. Laurel's father was not some ne'er do well surfer dude. He was a well-educated millionaire.

And what would she have told Nat about her second pregnancy—had he been around to tell? The truth. Gemma would've told her beloved brother the truth.

Having only a vague idea of where, in the cemetery, the Sommerset clan were buried, Gemma knew her first challenge would be to find Nat's grave. As children, the two of them had sometimes accompanied their father on Veterans Day, helping him place American flags beside the appropriate tombstones. But all she could remember from those visits was driving up a hill.

The minute she turned into the cemetery, it began to rain. Hesitating, she chose a curving road which rose gently upward.

A copse of ancient maples looked familiar, so she kept going. Then dearly wished she'd gone a different way.

Parked beside the road was a white Nissan, her father's car. It was empty, but her father was easy to spot. Holding a black umbrella, he was kneeling beside a tombstone, his forehead pressed against the granite.

Desperately wanting to give him his privacy, she nearly kept driving. Instead, worried he might recognize her car and realize she was running away from him, she parked in front of the Nissan. After struggling to open her umbrella, she approached her father through the wet grass.

"Daddy," she said softly.

When he didn't respond, she remembered he was losing his hearing.

She raised her voice. "Daddy." Still no response.

But then he turned around, his face streaked with tears. Never had she seen her father cry.

"Gemma," he said. "You came. You're here."

She nodded, unable to explain, even to herself, precisely *why* she was there. In her own way, she'd been telling Nat good-by for years. Nor did she feel compelled, at long last, to "pay her respects," whatever that meant. It was more that, after all this time, she was finally ready to see the tombstone with her brother's name on it.

As if he somehow knew this, her father, still on his knees, managed to move to one side, allowing her to see the inscription.

> Nathanial Owings Sommerset, Private, US Army
> April 10, 1946, Columbus, Ohio – January 1970, MIA, Vietnam

Nothing but the cold, hard facts. No mention of

how he'd tried not to go, why he'd ended up having to.

She took a deep breath, let it out.

"Can you help me, please?" Her father, gripping the tombstone, was trying to stand up.

She hurried to him, grabbed him under his arms.

"Not like that," he said. "Let go."

But when she released him, he fell, his forehead striking the granite, his glasses flying off. He ended up lying on his side in the wet grass.

"I'm so very sorry," she said. "I'll go for help."

"Don't you dare leave me like this," he snapped. "Just give me a minute."

Already there was an egg-shaped blue lump above his right eye.

"Are you concussed?" she said.

"No. I'm perfectly fine. I just need some help getting to my feet."

"Then tell me what to do."

He managed to sit up. "Pull," he said, holding out a hand.

She set her umbrella down in the grass. "Give me both hands," she said, and he did.

That was when a man in a yellow slicker appeared, reminding her of Nat's raincoat, also yellow, back when he was in kindergarten. But the man resembled Tim more than Nat; he had a football player's build.

With the stranger lifting from behind, and Gemma gripping her father's bony hands, the two of them were able to set him upright in the pouring rain.

"A guardian angel," Gemma said to the man. "Thank you!"

"Just looked like the two of you could use some help." He did a double take. "Mr. Sommerset? Is that you?"

"It is," her father said. "Gemma, could you please hand me my glasses?"

She picked them up. "They're broken. All my fault. You'll need to get new ones."

"It's Brian Walker, Mr. Sommerset," the man said. "I had you for junior English."

"Brian." Her father seemed pleased. "You're still working here?"

"Don't have to talk to anyone in this job. Suits me just fine."

"Brian's a poet. Brian, this is my daughter, Gemma."

"Pleased to meet you, Gemma," Brian said. "Your dad was my favorite teacher. Turned me on to E.E. Cummings."

Gemma guided her father to her own car and got him settled in the passenger seat so she could drive him home. Brian offered to follow them in the Nissan, but then her father, broken glasses in his lap, couldn't find his keys and sheepishly wondered if he might have left them in the ignition.

Brian dashed over to the car and discovered that this was indeed the case.

"Thanks for this," Gemma said to him as he prepared to get into her father's car. "I can give you a ride back to the cemetery afterwards."

"No need. I can hitchhike. Or take a bus."

Gemma insisted. "But it's raining."

Brian shrugged. "It's OK. This road circles back around to the entrance," he said. "I'll be right behind you."

The house where she and Nat had grown up never seemed to age. At her father's direction, she parked on the side street, giving Brian enough room to park directly behind her.

"Should we invite him in?" she said to her father.

"Your mother's not expecting company."

"I'm company," Gemma pointed out.

"The very best kind. You won't care if she's still in her nightgown."

Before helping her father out of her car, she walked back to the Nissan.

"I'll take my father inside," she said to Brian, "and then drive you back to the cemetery."

"Sure hope he's going to be OK," Brian said. "Your dad's one of the kindest people I know."

While guiding her father along the flagstone walk, she noticed that the boxwood hedges needed trimming. His house key was in the Nissan with his car keys, so she rang the doorbell.

It took a while for her mother, wearing a blue corduroy bathrobe, to open the door. "Gemma?" she said, as if she might be imagining things. "Is it really you?"

"Daddy needs ice," she said. "On his forehead. And new glasses. It's all my fault."

"Don't listen to her," he said. "I'm perfectly fine."

Gemma's call to Lexington to make arrangements for Laurel proved to be the easiest part of the long afternoon. A classmate's mother agreed to pick Laurel up from kindergarten, saying Laurel could spend the night if necessary.

"You can stay?" Her mother became weepy. "Oh, Gemma."

"For a while, yes. First, though, I need to drive someone back to the cemetery. Daddy will explain."

But the Nissan, with the keys in the ignition, was empty. Calling Brian's name, again and again, she hurried up to the street, hoping to spot him.

And then, feeling like a lost child, she just stood there, under her umbrella.

On the street where she'd grown up.

On the day her beloved brother would've turned fifty.

Cars splashed by. A neighbor with a red umbrella retrieved her mail.

No one even noticed Gemma or knew who she was.

Brian had somehow managed to disappear.

Sloshing through puddles, she walked back to her father's car. Gripping the steering wheel, mesmerized by raindrops following each other down the windshield, she allowed the awful truths to sink in.

Her parents were getting old.

They *were* old. They needed her.

Nat would've noticed.

His self-absorbed sister had not been paying attention.

Idling in the driveway of the basement-level garage, Gemma pushed the button on the remote attached to the Nissan's visor. It wasn't until the door began to open that she remembered: her parents parked on the street for a reason. The garage was so full of junk that there was no room in it for a car.

One more transgression on her part. Hadn't she promised her parents, years ago, to find someone to haul all that stuff away?

Choosing her path carefully, she made her way between pieces of furniture, cardboard boxes, rusted shovels, rolled-up rugs, broken flowerpots, and an ancient TV set. That she was able to open the door to the basement was a welcome surprise. As was the fact that the light switch still worked, illuminating the cement steps up to the kitchen.

She pressed the magic button on the wall. With a familiar, high-pitched screech, down came the garage door, separating the rain-spattered Nissan from its former home.

Having climbed the steps to the kitchen, she found the door locked. So she knocked in the pattern she and Nat had used as children: *Shave and a haircut, two bits.*

"Noooo," she heard her mother moan.

"Mother," Gemma called. "It's me."

The door opened slowly.

"Didn't mean to frighten you." Gemma stepped into the kitchen.

Maryl's cheeks were flushed. "It's just that no one has come up those basement steps in years," she said. "I thought you'd gone back to the cemetery."

"Brian must have hitched a ride. Where's Daddy?"

"Upstairs, changing his clothes."

Gemma propped her umbrella against the refrigerator, draped her raincoat on a chair. "OK if I use your phone?"

She left a message for Tim, said she was in Lynchburg and wasn't sure when she'd be home. Nothing to worry about, her parents were fine, and she'd made arrangements for Laurel to stay with a friend.

"I'm sorry," Gemma added. "I hope you can manage."

"Manage what?" her mother asked after she'd hung up.

Gemma explained. During tax season, Tim continued to count on her to greet his clients when they arrived, offer them coffee or whatever, then point them upstairs as the previous client was leaving. He claimed he was getting too old to make so many trips up and down the stairs in one night.

Seated in a kitchen chair, she removed her wet socks and shoes. "Do you maybe have some slippers I could wear?"

"I'll go up and find some."

"I'll go," Gemma said.

"You wouldn't know where to look."

"The floor of your closet?" Gemma said.

Her mother smiled. "That would be a good place to begin, yes."

As Gemma started up, her father was slowly coming down. His dark blue bathrobe matched the bruise on his forehead. With one hand gripping the sturdy oak banister, he pointed with the other to the sunglasses he was wearing.

"Prescription," he said. "Better than nothing."

In her mother's closet, a pair of turquoise Muk Luks looked familiar. And hadn't she once given her mother a matching bathrobe for Christmas? After locating the robe, she removed her damp slacks, hung them to dry over the heat vent in the bathroom, and, sporting turquoise from head to toe, went back downstairs.

In their various shades of blue, the three bathrobed Sommersets had lunch together in the kitchen. Gemma then helped to grate fresh coconut for the icing on a German chocolate cake.

Nat's favorite cake, to be baked by his mother, on his fiftieth birthday.

"Will you stay for dinner?" Maryl asked.

Not trusting her voice, Gemma nodded. She then hurried upstairs.

Her slacks were dry, so she put them on. Tiptoed into Nat's room. Sat down on his bed. Whispered to the full-length mirror on his closet door, "We miss you so much, Nat. All three of us do."

Back downstairs, she wandered over to the built-in bookshelves in the living room. Her parents had fewer books than Logan, but theirs were better organized. Shakespeare occupied the top two shelves. Below him were nineteenth- and twentieth-century writers, arranged alphabetically, from James Agee to Virginia Woolf.

Many of them were books her father had enjoyed teaching.

Noticing a protruding yellow bookmark, Gemma leaned down and removed *The Picture of Dorian Gray.* All she knew of Oscar Wilde was *The Importance of Being Earnest.* As a teenager, she'd seen the play with Fontana and her grandmother.

A penciled arrow on the bookmarked page was almost too faint to see. She turned on a table lamp and sat down on the sofa.

The sentence the arrow pointed to gave her chills: "*Children begin by loving their parents; as they grow older, they judge them; sometimes they forgive them.*"

Leaving the bookmark in place, she turned to the novel's first page.

It wasn't long before her father appeared, wearing slacks and a gray sweater, and asked his favorite question. "What're you reading?"

"*The Picture of Dorian Gray,*" she said.

"Ah. Gothic horror, with some typical Wilde humor mixed in. It's what saved him, you know, all his life, his sense of humor."

"I didn't know. Is this bookmark yours?"

"I don't think so." He took the book from her, sat down with it, and turned to the bookmarked page.

"The sentence was important to someone," she said. "See the arrow?"

"Not with these sunglasses, no. Can you read it to me?"

After taking a deep breath, she did.

"I know you blame me for your brother's death," he said softly. "And the truth is . . ." He took a breath. "I've come to blame myself. Haven't quite known how to tell you how very sorry I am. At the time, I thought I was doing the right thing."

"I just miss him so much."

"Of *course* you do. So do your mother and I." He seemed to be searching for the right words. "And we miss you, Gemma. Seems like you've kind of abandoned us lately."

"Well," Gemma said, "I have Laurel now. And so many grandchildren in Fairfax that I can't keep track." Keep track? What did that even mean? "I'll try to do better."

They sat in silence.

"A total non sequitur," her father said, "but I just re-membered what Oscar Wilde's last words were."

"Tell me," Gemma said.

"He was in Paris, living in exile, very sick, in a shab-by hotel, and he said, 'Either this wallpaper goes or I do.'"

"To whom?"

"Good question," her father replied. "I don't know who was there with him."

Gemma wondered where Nat had been, what he'd been thinking at the end, if he'd even been conscious and able to think.

"Mind if I join you?" Without waiting for an answer, Maryl, still in her bathrobe, sank down beside Gem-ma. "What're you two jabbering on about?"

"Oscar Wilde," Carson said. "How brilliant he was."

"I suppose." She turned to Gemma. "Cake's in the oven. Could you please take it out at 3:30? I'm going up for a nap."

Gemma looked at her watch. "Sure."

"Want to hear some Oscar Wilde first?" Carson said. "Gemma can read to us both."

"All right," Maryl said. "As long as it's PG-rated."

Gemma began at the beginning.

"The studio was filled with the rich color of roses, and when the light summer wind stirred amidst the trees of the garden there came through the open door the heavy scent of the lilac, or the more delicate perfume of the pink-flowering thorn.

From the corner of the divan of Persian saddle-bags on which he was lying, smoking, as usual, innumerable cigarettes, Lord Henry Wotton could just catch the gleam of the honey-sweet and honey-colored blossoms of the laburnum..."

Gemma stopped. Her mother, head thrown back, was snoring.

22

While Laurel's smile had a logical explanation, her fascination with Dalmatians was downright eerie. She'd never even seen the Disney movie.

She'd read the book, though, multiple times, having come across *One Hundred and One Dalmatians* in the public library, and then begged for a copy of her own. It was the illustrations she liked, more than the story. She began drawing Dalmatians herself, hundreds of them—in pencil at first, and then, as she got better at it, in black ink.

When Tim suggested giving her a Dalmatian puppy for Christmas, Gemma objected, insisting that Dalmatians were too inbred, too high-strung. Why not get Laurel a lovable mutt instead?

"What on earth makes you think Dalmatians are hyper?" Tim said. "Have you ever actually seen one?"

Gemma shook her head.

A Gorgeous lie.

Noreen found a breeder in Frederick, Maryland, from whom Tim, a few days before Christmas, purchased a puppy.

Christmas Day, 2000, began with Laurel pulling gifts from a Santa she no longer believed in from the stocking she had nevertheless hung from the mantle the night before. Tim then quietly left through the kitchen door, drove over to a friend's house, and returned with the puppy.

How happy he'd been that morning! Over-the-moon proud of himself.

When she saw the puppy, Laurel burst into tears. "But you said there weren't any Dalmatians around here," she blubbered.

"Your sister found an ad in the *Washington Post*," Tim said.

"Noreen? She doesn't much like dogs."

"But she likes you." Tim put the dog down on the living room rug. "What do you want to name her?"

"I don't know." Laurel held out her hand, and the puppy licked her palm.

"What about Dolly?" Tim said. "Dolly the Dalmatian."

Laurel seemed to be thinking this over.

"Hi, Dolly," she whispered.

And Dolly peed on the rug.

*   *   *

A week later—on New Year's Day, 2001—Gemma was sitting in the living room with a cup of coffee. For months, she'd been planning to greet the first sunrise of the new millennium from her chair on the deck. Instead, she'd slept right through it.

Furious with herself, she sat glaring at the unlit Christmas tree, the empty stockings. Christmas was over, and, for her anyway, New Year's Day was already a complete bust.

A loud thump from upstairs made her wonder what Tim had dropped on the floor. She didn't bother to call up to him, didn't ask if he was OK.

Laurel was outside, walking a possible distant relative of Gorgeous.

While searching the internet for any mention of a Logan Rhodes in California, Gemma had discovered an obituary for his wife. According to the *San Francisco Chronicle*, Patricia Rhodes had been preceded in death by a daughter, Margaret. In lieu of flowers, contributions could be made to the American Cancer Society.

Not long after coming across the obituary, Gemma had dreamed that she and Laurel were in Carmel. When they knocked on the front door of Laurel Cottage, they were greeted by a girl who could've been Laurel's identical twin. Same smile, with Logan's beautiful teeth.

While Gemma and Laurel stood there, waiting to be asked in, the girl's lips turned purple. Her eyes liquefied and ran down her cheeks.

That she was remembering a nightmare on the first day of the new millennium gave Gemma chills. She finished her coffee, took the empty cup to the kitchen, and went upstairs to get dressed.

Tim was lying on his back, on the floor beside their bed. His eyes were open, staring up at the ceiling. He was wearing his Christmas present from his sister in Florida, boxer shorts in a green-and-red plaid.

Gemma shouted Tim's name, leaned down and pinched his arm. He didn't respond.

Two thoughts circled around in her head. She'd never seen a dead person before. She did not want the first one to be Tim.

She wondered if she should try to close his eyes. Instead, she dialed 911.

"Daddy's had an accident," she said when Laurel and Dolly returned. "I called for help."

"He's going to the hospital?" Laurel said.

"I think so. Maybe."

"Then he'll be OK?"

"I don't know." A lie. Tim's father's heart attack had been fatal. "Better put Dolly in her crate."

"But she hasn't had breakfast yet."

"Then put her feed bowl in the crate, too."

Gemma and Laurel waited in the upstairs hallway while two EMTs examined Tim. It didn't take long. One of them came out and said, "Probably a heart attack." He then shook his head. "I'm so sorry."

Laurel didn't move, didn't react.

"Tell her to breathe," the man said. "Deep breaths."

"I want to see him," Laurel said.

When Gemma nodded, the man took Laurel's hand. "Your Daddy's gone to heaven," he said.

"Can I kiss him goodbye?"

"OK by me."

Standing over Tim, Laurel raised her right hand to her mouth. After kissing her fingers, she bent down to touch his forehead, as if bestowing a ritual blessing.

Gemma then followed her daughter's example, hoping for a miracle, a response from Tim.

Nothing.

His forehead was cold. He really was dead.

She'd heard the thump. So why hadn't she gone upstairs? Instead, she'd just sat there, thinking about Logan, and Gorgeous, and the horrible nightmare.

One technician made a phone call from the bedroom, while the other followed Gemma and Laurel downstairs. There were forms to be filled out. Gemma led him to the kitchen table and offered him coffee, which he declined.

"Hey, there," he said to Dolly, who clearly wanted out of her crate. "A fire dog!"

"Daddy gave her to me for Christmas," Laurel said.

"I'm glad you'll have a friend," the man said. "Friends are important."

After the silent ambulance drove away with Tim's body, Laurel let Dolly out of the crate.

"I may be in shock," Gemma said. No tears had arrived, no feelings of any sort. "Come sit on my lap."

"I'm too big for that," Laurel said.

"Please, honey."

"But Brenda's here," Laurel whispered.

And there, at the back door, was their next-door neighbor, Brenda. An older woman, a widow. Gemma went to the door but didn't open it.

"Tim," she mouthed through the glass.

"So sorry," Brenda called out. "Anything I can do?"

Gemma shook her head. "I'll let you know," she said. One widow to another.

Brenda nodded. She gave a small wave and retreated down the back-porch steps.

From the kitchen phone, Gemma dialed Noreen's number in Fairfax, forgetting that Noreen and her family were in Kentucky with Marshall's parents.

When she called Lynchburg, her mother answered on the second ring.

"Tim had a heart attack," Gemma managed. "This morning."

"We'll be right up," her mother said.

"No need. He's." She couldn't say the word. "They. Took. Him. Away."

"We'll leave in ten minutes."

Gemma caught her breath, managed to make a request. "Could you call Tim's mother, in Florida, first? Tell her Laurel and I are OK. One sec." Gemma put the phone down, found the number in Tallahassee, picked the phone up again.

"Got it," Maryl said, and they hung up.

"I'm not OK," Laurel said. "I'm pissed."

Gemma held out her arms, and Laurel walked into them.

I heard a thud, she wanted to confess to her daughter. *Should've gone up to investigate.*

Instead, she made room in her soul for yet another guilty secret.

A financially cautious man, Tim had left a will. Like most wills, it didn't specify what to do with the body.

"He wanted to be cremated," Gemma told his mother on the phone.

"Are you sure? He never said anything like that to me."

"Positive. Laurel heard him, too."

They'd been in a canoe, on the South Fork of the Shenandoah River, under the center span of a bridge, when Tim announced, his voice echoing, "I want my ashes scattered right here. It reminds me of something."

The trestles, he'd meant. "But that was a railroad bridge," Gemma had reminded him.

"Doesn't matter. Promise me, OK?"

"All right," she'd said. "As Laurel is our witness."

The funeral was held in the small church in Buena Vista where Tim's father had delivered Sunday sermons. Tim's mother and sister flew up from Tallahassee. So many came to pay their respects that the pews filled up quickly, with latecomers left standing in the aisles. While his mother Noreen wept in the front row, his daughter Noreen, who was pregnant again, stepped up to the pulpit and sang "Will the Circle Be Unbroken?"

At his mother's insistence, most of Tim's ashes were buried in the family plot in Buena Vista. Gemma had carefully spooned the rest into the bright blue Jim Beam decanter Tim had kept on his desk. On the front of the bottle was a reproduction of a painting by Frederic Remington—a man astride a horse.

On a beautiful Saturday in late March, Gemma and Laurel paddled off in a rented canoe, heading north on the South Fork of the Shenandoah. Just the two of them because Noreen, who'd been planning to come, had reluctantly decided she was too pregnant to spend hours in a canoe.

The South Fork flowed into the Shenandoah, which continued on to join the Potomac at Harper's Ferry.

Gemma was worried she might not recognize the bridge Tim had chosen. Or that his bridge had since been replaced with a completely different structure.

"Do ashes float?" Laurel called from the bow. "Or do they sink?"

"I guess we'll find out."

"If they float, then Daddy could go all the way to Washington, DC."

"And from there to the Chesapeake Bay."

After they'd been paddling for what seemed like

entirely too long, Gemma pointed to a bridge in the distance. "Do you think that's it?"

"Yesss!" Laurel said. "That's it, all right."

In the center of the bridge's shadow, Gemma stowed her paddle and unscrewed the cap on the flask. "Do you want to go first?"

Laurel shook her head.

"Should we say something?" Gemma said.

"I wish Noreen was here to sing."

"So do I," Gemma said. "But you can do that, if you want."

Laurel seemed to be thinking this over.

"OK," she said. "You pour. I'll sing."

Gemma made curvy S patterns in the water. Some of the ashes sank, some floated away.

And Laurel sang. A Dolly Parton song.

"'I will always love you. Yes, I will always love you.'"

During their return trip, against the current, Laurel called back from the bow.

"What are cemeteries for, anyway?"

Gemma had always wondered this herself. "So that families will remember?"

"They're not going to forget."

"It's what people have been doing since the beginning of time," Gemma said. "Burying their dead. Paying their respects."

"I like what we did better."

"Yes," Gemma said. "It's what he said he wanted."

23

Most of Gemma's friends in Lexington had sensed, correctly, that she preferred to be left alone. So she was surprised when, late one afternoon, the doorbell rang.

Through the window in the front door, Gemma could see a Black woman. Nina's mother? Ever since Tim died, Laurel had been spending nearly every afternoon with her friend Nina, whose father, James, in an eerie coincidence, had died in an automobile accident not long after Tim's fatal heart attack.

Laurel and Nina liked to visit Evergreen, Lexington's Black cemetery, where James was buried.

"What do you do there?" Gemma had asked.

"Sit by his grave," Laurel had replied with a shrug.

"Do you talk?"

"Of course."

"About what?"

"Nothing you'd be interested in."

"Does Nina know you learned to walk in a cemetery?"

"Why would she even care?"

Gemma remembered conversations like this with her own mother.

After taking a deep breath, she opened the front door.

"I'm Yvonne Sawyer," the woman said. "Nina's mother."

"Are the girls all right?" Gemma asked in alarm.

"Oh, yes. I'm sure they are. I just wanted to stop by, finally, that's all. Hope you don't mind."

"Of course not," Gemma said. "Come on in."

"I won't stay long."

"You can stay as long as you'd like. I'll make some tea. Or would you prefer coffee?"

"No need," Yvonne said. "But thanks. I don't react well to caffeine."

"Herbal tea?" Gemma offered.

"That would be great." Yvonne followed Gemma into the kitchen.

"Let me get these dirty dishes off the table," Gemma said, "before you sit down."

"I can clear the table," Yvonne said, and she did.

Gemma opened a cabinet door. "Let's see. Vanilla, Peppermint, or Black Cherry? Sounds like I'm offering you ice cream."

"I'll try the Black Cherry." Yvonne raised her eyebrows. "I thought we might get along, was hoping we would. Laurel's been *such* a good friend to Nina." She sat down at the table. "I'm so very glad they have each other. Are you doing OK?"

"I guess." Gemma filled the teapot with water. "Not really. It's only been, what, four months? What about you?"

"Not really," Yvonne admitted. "But we'll get through this."

"The girls seem to have found their own way of coping."

"I think it's that they know no one will bother them at Evergreen," Yvonne said. "If they were visiting your husband's grave, then someone might come up and ask Nina to leave. In Evergreen, they're both safe."

Gemma explained that most of Tim's ashes had been buried in Buena Vista, not Lexington. And the rest scattered from a canoe.

"So you divvied him up." Yvonne smiled. "Well, James is all in one place. And I'm really glad Laurel is helping Nina tell him good-bye. Even though it seems to be taking forever." She looked at her watch. "They've probably started home by now. I usually pick them up somewhere along the way."

"We could let them walk all the way here," Gemma

said. "I have leftover spaghetti sauce, for dinner."

"Another time, maybe," Yvonne said. "We'd love that."

It didn't happen. At the end of the school year, Yvonne and Nina moved to Baltimore, where they had family. After that, Laurel never saw her friend again.

With Tim, Gemma had seen him lying there, so very still, on the bedroom floor. She'd watched the silent ambulance take him away. She'd gone to his funeral and, months later, sprinkled his ashes under a bridge.

She knew he was dead.

Just as with Nat, though, there was guilt. If only she'd gone upstairs, the minute she'd heard the thump, Tim might have lived.

Still, someone you'd loved was never really gone. Instead, that person became present in an entirely new way. Silently reminding you. Hanging around.

Two years after Tim died, her parents, too, became hoverers. Her father went first, and then, two months later, her mother followed him into the great beyond.

Although they'd been in different nursing homes,

Gemma had noticed alarmingly similar problems. Mix-ups in medications. Poor communication between the caregivers and the administrative staff. Rigid policies that did more harm than good.

"Your mother has lost so much weight," a visiting doctor said to Gemma. "It's good you can be here at lunchtime. It's probably the only meal she eats."

"I'm so sorry about what happened," said one of her father's doctors. "Your dad should never have been given that dosage."

Gemma had considered moving to Lynchburg temporarily but didn't want Laurel to have to change schools and then change back again. Instead, on weekday mornings, she dropped Laurel off at school and drove to Lynchburg, returning to Lexington by the time school let out. An exhausting routine, which did little to dispel the guilt that she wasn't doing enough for her parents.

Early one morning, not long after her mother's funeral, Gemma was on the deck in Lexington for the first time in what seemed like years. As the sun tinted the sky in shades of lavender and peach, she made a solemn promise to herself: never, ever would she let anyone put her in a nursing home. Death was preferable to that sort of life. She would spare her daughters the agony.

Her parents' house had grown old with them. With the house, though, Gemma at least knew what to do, how to help. Sort through their possessions, then arrange for most of the stuff to be hauled away. Give the place a thorough cleaning.

While in a Lynchburg grocery story one morning, she ran into a high school classmate. Their senior year, Pam had been Homecoming Queen. Gemma didn't remember seeing Pam at either Maryl's or Carson's funeral and so was surprised to hear her mention them.

"I'm so sorry about your parents," Pam said, eyeing the Ajax and Lysol and colored sponges in Gemma's grocery cart. "I know what you're going through."

"It's been difficult, yes," Gemma said. "Right now, I'm trying to get their house ready to put on the market."

"There are cleaning services here, you know," Pam said. "I use Maids Kincaid."

"Thanks. Maybe I'll give them a call." But she knew she wouldn't. Cleaning the house felt like something she should do herself.

"Still in touch with Fontana?" Pam asked.

Gemma shook her head. "Last time I saw her, she said she might be moving to Alaska."

"Alaska! That's Fontana for you. Miss Adventure."

Pam, who'd married one of the football players, wasn't wearing a wedding ring. Her grocery cart contained salad greens and a few cartons of yogurt.

Gemma chose a mop and set it down in her own cart. With the mop's wooden handle looking like a mast, she prepared to set sail.

"Wonderful to see you again, Pam. Please, stop by the house, any time you'd like."

"Will do," Pam said.

But of course, she didn't.

The most valuable find in her parents' house was a box on the top shelf of her mother's closet. In it were the letters her father had written home while stationed in Japan.

And the letters her mother had faithfully written to him? Nowhere to be found. Probably hadn't been saved in the first place.

Japan! The travel writer had never even considered writing about a foreign country.

24

When Laurel went off to college, to the University of Pennsylvania, Gemma was, for the first time in her life, completely alone. No husband or daughters, no parents or brother in the house. No one but Dolly, who seemed to miss Laurel as much as Gemma did.

They took long walks together, usually along the Woods Creek Trail. *A trail (duh) next to a creek (duh) in the woods (duh)*, Laurel had drily observed when she was five. Gemma had subsequently learned that the creek was probably named after an early settler named Richard Woods.

Lexington, with its thousands of mature trees, was a woodsy paradise for deer, the creek a popular watering hole. Straining at her leash, Dolly would bark wildly at the deer, who calmly ignored her.

What Dolly so very badly wanted (or so it seemed to Gemma), was to join the herd. Break free of the human-who-was-not-Laurel and spend her days with more exciting friends.

Occasionally, in response to Dolly's rude behavior, a doe would look up, stare at the dog, and then return to her grazing.

"They're not interested," Gemma would say to Dolly. "Looks like you're stuck with me."

As for the antlered stag they sometimes encountered at dusk, Dolly would simply freeze, silent as a statue. Gemma, too, was in awe of his royal demeanor.

Walking through the woods, by the creek, didn't make either of them less lonely. For Gemma, though, it was a reminder of happier times. She greeted the trees she could identify as if they were old friends. Took photographs of species she didn't recognize, then looked them up when she got home.

It wasn't the Limberlost, with its sacred hemlocks, but then nothing ever would be again. She befriended a spectacular sugar maple and an ancient hickory. Spent time gazing up into their branches.

Occasionally, one of the does would look at Gemma with what seemed like recognition. Elated, barely breathing, Gemma would fix her gaze on its soft brown eyes.

One afternoon, while standing at the kitchen sink, Gemma realized that Dolly had come in and was lying with her chin resting on Gemma's sneakers. That Dolly had never, ever done this before should have set off an alarm. Instead, Gemma simply thought: *How sweet!*

It was months before she took the dog to the vet. He anesthetized Dolly, opened her up, and discovered the problem.

Liver cancer. Incurable.

A dog's death is far more humane than a human's. Euthanasia is both legal and desirable. Why should an animal be required to suffer?

Laurel was in the middle of exams at Penn. When Gemma finally reached her, there were long pauses during which neither of them could speak. Between sobs, they decided to have Dolly cremated.

"We'll scatter her ashes in Woods Creek," Laurel managed to say.

Gemma wondered if this was even legal.

"Maybe they'll get as far as the Maury," Laurel blubbered on. "And even the James. She could end up with Daddy in the Chesapeake Bay."

That summer, after she and Laurel had sprinkled Dolly's ashes at several points along Woods Creek, after Laurel had returned to Philadelphia, Gemma began going down to Woods Creek Trail nearly every evening.

The trees seemed to welcome her, as did the deer.

Communing with a deer became the highlight of her day. A three- or four-deer day made her heart soar. The evenings when she didn't see a single pair of large brown eyes, or even a white tail bounding away from her, brought on something very close to despair.

One evening, as she was heading down the hill, there was a commotion in the woods beside her. A doe, going lickety-split, was soaring over any obstacles in her path—dead branches, boulders, tree stumps. Neither chasing nor being chased, she was instead simply kicking up her heels, having herself a grand old time.

Soaring through the air, as if suddenly aware of who she was and could become.

Don't forget this, Gemma called softly to the doe. *Don't you ever forget!*

Part IV

Truth and Consequences

25

When the phone rang, that fateful night, Gemma nearly let the answering machine in the kitchen record a message. Instead, on the off chance that it might be one of her daughters calling, she fumbled for the receiver and said, "Hello."

"Gemma?" a male voice said. "Is this Gemma?"

"Who's calling please?" she snapped.

"Hope I didn't wake you," the man said. "Just realized. My watch is still on west coast time."

She waited.

"Gemma, it's Logan. Logan Rhodes."

She sat up. Felt for the lamp on the bedside table. Managed to turn it on.

"I'm in Richmond," he said. "Thought maybe we could have lunch or something."

"Richmond, *Virginia*?"

"My cousin's getting married. He asked me to be his best man. And, well, I'd never been to Richmond."

"How did you find me?"

"You gave me your business card, with a phone

number, remember? I keep it behind my driver's license. I was worried the number would belong to someone else by now."

All these years, he'd had her phone number?

"The wedding's tomorrow, Saturday," he went on. "I fly back on Monday."

"To Carmel?"

"San Francisco. I'm renting the cottage out for a while."

Remembering the little girl in her nightmare, Gemma wanted to ask who the renters were.

"You still there?" Logan said.

"Yes. This is just such a surprise."

"I have a rental car. I think I can find my way to Lexington. On Sunday. Would that be convenient for you?"

The house was a mess. She'd have a day to clean it up. "Sunday. Yes."

"We can go to your favorite restaurant."

"Logan. Is it really you?"

"Twenty years older but no wiser," he said.

"What time on Sunday?"

"How long a drive is it?"

"Scenic route or interstate?" she said.

"Interstate would be faster?"

"Yes, about two hours that way." She gave him her

address.

"So Google had that right. I'll plan to be there around one."

Having barely slept, she was in the kitchen the next morning before dawn, staring at the Blue Ridge Parkway wall calendar while her coffee brewed. The only notation for the month of May was a reminder about a granddaughter's birthday. In the square for Sunday, May 15, 2011, she scribbled, in blue ink: *L.R. 1:00.*

After filling her trusty thermos, she climbed the steps to the deck and settled into her chair. She would see Logan again, and then he'd leave. She would tell him about Laurel, or she wouldn't.

Despite the coffee, she felt a chill. How extensive had his Google searching been? Did he know her husband had died?

Her thoughts in a swirl, she watched as the sky began to lighten, treating her to a magnificent sunrise, which she refused to see as an omen. She continued to sit there, her mind in turmoil, until she heard dogs barking, children calling out to one another on a Saturday morning.

Tapping the rickety railing, as if for good luck, she made her way down the steps. Then spent the morning vacuuming and dusting the downstairs. Cleaning the half-bath. Mopping the kitchen floor for the first time that year.

No need to bother with the upstairs. They would have lunch, then say good-bye, and life would go on.

But have lunch where? She hadn't kept up with Lexington's restaurant scene. Whenever she didn't feel like cooking, she went to a Chinese place, friendly folks who didn't mind seating a single woman. Then returned home with leftovers for dinner the following night.

Realizing that for someone living in San Francisco, Chinese food would be old hat, she called to make reservations at the historic Sheridan Livery Inn. When a recording encouraged her to leave a message, she panicked and hung up, worried Logan might be late, or change his mind and not show up at all.

As nervous as a teenager with an important date, she stood at the front window, imagining his arrival. Going out to his car to greet him, she decided, would make her appear far too eager. Instead, she would wait for him to knock on the door.

And then what?

While they were hugging or shaking hands or awk-wardly saying hello, Logan might notice the large family photo on the wall. Three generations—Gemma and Tim and their two daughters, plus Carson and Maryl—in a massive mahogany frame.

With some effort, Gemma took the photo down and stowed it in the hall closet. Upstairs, in the girls' room, she found a smaller photo, one she had taken herself. Laurel, who'd been in middle school at the time, was kneeling in the snow, cupping Dolly's chin in her hands in such a way that the dog, too, seemed to be smiling.

Having hung the photo in its new location, Gemma stepped back, wondering which would be more likely to grab Logan's attention—a Dalmatian, or his daughter's smile? If he even noticed the photo. If he did notice, and was curious enough to ask about the girl and the Dalmatian, then Gemma would tell him the truth.

Somehow, she would find the words.

At a quarter past one on Sunday afternoon, a white car pulled into the driveway. Gemma watched, from behind the living room curtains, as the car door opened.

His hair was white. He was wearing khakis and a blue plaid shirt. Eerily similar to the shirt he'd been wearing that day in the Carmel Library.

She waited for him to knock, then opened the door.

He stepped inside, put his arms around her. "Are we alone?"

She nodded, and he gave her a quick kiss.

"How was the wedding?" she said.

"Exhausting. I was the oldest one there."

"Was it a big wedding?"

He was staring at the photo. "That can't be Gorgeous."

"Her name was Dolly." So this was how it would happen. "My younger daughter's dog."

He staggered, then reached for her shoulder. "Sorry. Too much champagne last night."

"Can I get you some water?"

"Please. We've never been friends, champagne and I. Had to drink it, though, being best man and all."

She closed the front door. Took his arm, started down the hall to the kitchen.

"Ah. Just what I need. May I?" He stepped into the half bath and shut the door.

When he finally reappeared, she was waiting in the kitchen doorway with a glass of water. "Logan?"

"There you are." He smiled, came toward her. "I guess I never told you. My grandfather was Logan. My friends call me Low."

"L-o?"

"L-o-w. As in Low Rhodes. What I usually take, the

implication was, as opposed to the high roads. Got any aspirin?"

She offered him Tylenol, explained that she could no longer take aspirin.

"Tylenol's no help with headaches." He took the glass of water from her, drank half of it, then sat down at the kitchen table. "Mind if I sit down?"

Logan Rhodes—mystery man, long-lost father of her second child—was sitting in her kitchen. "Are you hungry?" she said. "I could scramble some eggs."

"A bowl of cereal, maybe? All I've had today is coffee."

"I think I have Kix. Maybe some Raisin Bran."

He gave her a look. "I haven't had Kix in years."

"Coming right up, then. But Logan? I'm going to stick with Logan."

He shrugged, drank the rest of the water. "You live here by yourself?"

She set a bowl of Kix in front of him along with a carton of milk. "My husband died."

"I know. Google is a terrible invader of privacy. I'm so sorry."

She'd never told anyone.

She sat down and said, "Remember when Humbert Humbert realized Lolita was gone? And he ran outside the motel—frantic, hoping to see her—but there was no Lo to behold?"

"Vaguely. Maybe."

"That's why I can't call you Lo."

"I don't care what you call me." He swallowed some cereal. "What did you think of that book?"

"He was sick and evil and twisted, but he loved her." He shrugged.

"Logan?"

"Yes?"

"There's something I need to tell you."

"All right."

"Not telling you would be lying."

"Then go ahead."

"My younger daughter, the girl in the photo with the Dalmatian? Did you notice her smile?"

"What about it?"

Gemma stood up, left the kitchen, and returned with the photo.

"She's pretty. What's her name?"

"Laurel."

"I give up. Tell me."

"She was born in January of 1991."

He stared at the pink dogwood in full bloom outside the kitchen window. "So?"

"Do the math, Logan. She's your daughter."

Now he was staring at her. "But I thought."

"I thought so, too. That I couldn't get pregnant. Tim and I had been trying for years, and then we stopped, because it was just so hard to keep on failing, and he blamed me, but it turned out I could, and I did, and if you'd ever written to me, or called, I mean you could've done both of those things, but you didn't, then I would've told you."

Logan was staring out the window again.

"I tried to call you once," she said, "but Information had no listing in Carmel for a Logan Rhodes. I wanted to tell you. It seemed wrong not to. But I didn't want to put it in writing. Where your wife might see it."

"The phone in Carmel is an unlisted number." He took her hand.

"She's smart, Logan. She's at the University of Pennsylvania, on a full scholarship. All her life, she's been crazy about Dalmatians."

He was staring at the photo.

"She has your smile," Gemma said softly.

"I had a daughter," he said. "She died. From leukemia. She was only ten."

"I'm so sorry."

He let go of her hand. "My wife and I couldn't handle it, not together, that's why I was in Carmel alone."

"I thought her mother had had a stroke."

"That, too. I never lied to you, Gemma. I just didn't

tell you the whole truth."

"You and I, we hardly know each other at all."

"Then my wife died," he said. "Also from cancer. It ran in her family."

I know, Gemma could have said. "I'm sorry," she said instead.

"Did you ever tell your husband the child wasn't his?"

"Didn't have to," Gemma said. "We hadn't had sex for years."

"And he was OK with it?"

"Tim had always wanted another child."

"Tim had been sleeping around, too, was that it?"

"'Sleeping around?' That's what you call it?"

"Sorry. Poor choice of words." He took a bite of Kix. Chewed. Swallowed. "Do you think I could meet her? She wouldn't have to know, not if you don't want her to."

"Maybe sometime. There's a scrapbook you can look at, baby pictures up through high school graduation."

"She was born here, in Lexington?"

Gemma told him about going into labor, two weeks early, at Monticello. About having to stay in the hospital, in Charlottesville, till Laurel weighed five pounds.

"What would you have named her if she'd been a boy?"

Gemma shrugged. "Laurel."

"Jeez, Gemma. Good thing you had a girl."

"That's what everyone said."

"What did you tell Tim about me?"

"Only that I'd met you on the beach. He figured you for a beach bum."

Finally, that smile of his.

"I never let on that you were the exact opposite."

"Oh, Gemma. The money was all hers. My wife's." Logan finished his cereal and pushed the bowl aside. "I married up, as they say. Way up." He went to the sink, refilled his water glass.

She opened a cupboard, took down a cereal bowl, filled it with Kix.

"I promised you lunch," Logan said. "Let's go to lunch."

"This is so much better," she said. "Truly it is. Besides, we've never had breakfast together."

"Of course we have."

"You preferred to have breakfast alone, remember?"

"Not the day we went to Big Sur, remember?" Logan cocked his head. "Are you still a travel writer?"

She shook her head. "I kinda gave up on it. Lately, though, I've been reading books by great travel writers, hoping to learn from them."

"Lawrence Durrell," Logan said.

"And Peter Matthiessen and Paul Theroux. But also

travel books by women. They're not so well known. *Io-nia,* by Freya Stark, is fantastic."

Logan shook his head. "Never heard of her."

They were seated on the living room sofa. Logan had the scrapbook in his lap.

"Not entirely sure about this," he said. "She's mine but not mine."

"All right. You don't have to."

"I think I'd rather see her in person. She's in Philadelphia?"

"You know about her. She doesn't know about you."

"Maybe I could just get a glimpse of her from a distance."

"Spy on her, you mean?"

"Why not?" Logan put the scrapbook aside.

Gemma opened it and turned to the last page. "Senior prom." She pointed to a picture. "She has your smile."

Logan glanced at the photo, then looked away.

"Tim was a wonderful father to her," Gemma said. "She loved him. I'm not sure we should ruin that for her."

"Then why did you even tell me about her, if you don't want me to meet her?"

"Telling you about Laurel was the easy part." Gemma touched his arm. "Telling Laurel about you is something we would need to handle with great care."

"Maybe we could discuss it at dinner? Do you have a favorite restaurant?"

"It's Chinese."

"Haven't had Chinese in years," Logan said.

26

When they walked in, Gemma's favorite waitress, Ella, widened her eyes. Never before had Gemma arrived with a man.

Once they were seated, at Gemma's usual table, Logan ordered a Singapore Sling.

"Pinot Grigio for you?" Emma said, and Gemma nodded.

"To Singapore." Logan raised his water glass to her. "I've always wanted to go to Singapore."

"Is it anywhere near Japan?" Gemma felt as giddy as if she'd already drained her wineglass. "I wish I knew more about that part of the world. My father was stationed in Japan, after World War II ended."

"Japan's closer to Korea than to Singapore, I think. If you have a world atlas at home, we can look it up."

Gemma nodded. "I have all my parents' books."

Ella brought their drinks and took their orders.

"My father wrote wonderful letters home, to my mother," Gemma babbled on. "From Japan."

Logan tasted his Singapore Sling. "Excellent. A truly

excellent Singapore Sling in Virginia. Who would've guessed?"

Gemma took a long sip of wine. It went right to her head. She took a deep breath, then another sip.

"My grandfather went to Washington and Lee," Logan said. "That's why I was a little late today. I spent some time driving around the campus, trying to imagine him there."

So he'd had multiple reasons for coming to Virginia. Those annoying chimes in "The Twilight Zone" theme song rang in her ears, as if she'd entered Rod Serling's fifth dimension, where anything at all could happen.

Keeping it real, she stated an actual, historical fact. "Traveller's buried at Washington and Lee," she said. "His bones are, anyway."

"Who?"

"Traveller. Robert E. Lee's horse. I'd always hoped to use his name in one of my travel articles. Traveller's name, I mean. With two l's."

Ella, her eyes lowered, brought their dinners. They ate in silence.

"I was hungry," Gemma said.

"Me, too," Logan said. "We never had lunch. My fault entirely."

She finished her wine. The ringing in her ears had stopped.

"Does the expression 'chow down' come from Chinese?" she said.

"I have no idea," Logan said. "Do you want to ask your friend?"

"How can you tell we're friends?"

"The way you smile at each other."

As if on cue, Ella appeared. "Dessert?" she said. "Or fortune cookies?"

"Fortune cookies." They said this in unison.

"Take home?" she said, as she always did, and Gemma nodded, as usual, at what was left on the serving plates.

The cookies arrived, along with their bill, and Logan gave Ella a credit card. He then carefully chose a cookie, broke it open, and removed the strip of paper. "Japanese food makes you sick as a dog," he said.

"Very funny," Gemma said. "What does it really say?"

He squinted. "Be kind to pigeons. Someday you may be a statue."

Gemma grabbed the fortune from him. He'd read it correctly. She burst out laughing.

And couldn't stop. Tears ran down her cheeks.

"Gemma," Logan said. "What's wrong?"

She shook her head. As children, she and Nat had often laughed till they cried. But this felt different, as if a burden had been lifted. Logan knew. After all these years, she'd been able to tell him.

Ella returned with his credit card, along with two new fortune cookies. "Sometimes fortunes not worth reading." She set the cookies down. "Here. Try again."

Logan stared at the cookies. "Do we dare?"

Gemma dabbed at her eyes with her napkin. "You go first."

He crumbled a cookie and extracted its fortune. "'Never do anything halfway,'" he read.

She picked up the other cookie and broke it open. "Not even remotely possible," she said.

"Read it," Logan said. "You have to. Read it. Out loud."

"'Never do anything halfway.'" She handed him the strip of paper.

"We should report this to the authorities," he said.

"To the fortune police, you mean?"

He smiled his smile. "I'm scheduled to fly back to San Francisco tomorrow, from Richmond. Would it be all right if I stay here for a few days instead?"

In Lexington? In her house? In her bed?

"We need some time to talk this over," he said. "Think it through. If I'm Laurel's father…"

"You are."

"Then maybe I shouldn't meet her until we—you

and I—figure out where I might fit in."

Exactly! she thought. "All right," she said.

As they were leaving, Gemma gave Ella a small wave. Ella responded with a thumbs up.

Back home, Gemma motioned to the sofa. "Please. Sit down for a minute. I need to straighten up upstairs."

"Not necessary." Logan sat. "You weren't expecting an overnight guest. I'll sleep here."

"Not necessary. There are two bedrooms and three beds up there. Give me five minutes, maybe ten."

"All right." He stood up. "I'll call the airline, change my tickets."

The question was: *where* they would sleep. Together, in the master bedroom? Or apart, with Logan in the girls' room?

Noreen's bed had only a pillow and spread on it, but Laurel's bed was fully made up.

In the girls' bathroom, Gemma splashed water in the basin. She hung clean towels on the racks.

Ditto for the "master" bath.

In the bedroom she'd shared with Tim, she gathered clothes carelessly draped over chairs and hung them in the closet. She made space on the closet floor for several pairs of her shoes.

By then, she'd come up with a plan. She would offer Logan the opportunity to sleep in his daughter's bed. If he seemed relieved, well then, that's where he would spend the night. If not, well then, Laurel's biological parents would, once again, share a bed.

But Logan, she discovered, was way ahead of her. With his head on a throw pillow, his shoes off, he was fast asleep in his clothes on the sofa.

Near his feet lay an Afghan Gemma's Ohio grandmother had crocheted. The colorful flowers against a black background had spent decades folded over the arm of her parents' sofa in Lynchburg. Gently, so as not to wake him, Gemma covered Logan with it.

"Night, night," she whispered.

He didn't stir.

After making sure the doors were locked, after turning out all the lights except the one in the half bath, she tiptoed upstairs.

27

Despite a restless night, Gemma woke before dawn. She dressed quickly, then tiptoed downstairs.

The light in the bathroom had been turned off. Logan, lying on top of the Afghan, was snoring softly.

She stood there wondering: *had he always snored? Had she simply not noticed? How well did she actually know this man?*

Moving quietly around the kitchen, she brewed twice as much coffee as usual. Then filled her trusty thermos, left a note for Logan beside an empty cup, and climbed the steps to the deck in the dark.

Due to shifting clouds, the sunrise that morning was an on again, off-again affair.

A thought that, once she'd realized she'd thought it, made her smile.

Were she and Logan on again?

If so, then what should Laurel be told? And by whom?

If not, then why should Laurel be told anything at

all?

Your father and I lied to you would, in one sense, be factually incorrect, since Tim was not Laurel's biological father.

I lied to you. I've been lying to you for years. I also lied to Noreen. All were completely true. Brutally honest. Nearly impossible for a mother to say. Devastating for a daughter to hear.

Startled by a noise behind her, she turned around. Logan was trying to open the window in the girls' room.

"It sticks," she called to him. "Just yell."

"Didn't know where you were," he shouted.

"I left a note for you in the kitchen. Get some coffee and come join me."

"OK if I take a shower first?"

She nodded.

Feeling unsettled, she gazed up at the towering sycamore and the wise old oak, longtime friends whose patient wisdom she'd relied on for years. On this momentous morning in May, however, the giant trees seemed content to relinquish their hold on her to the seemingly fragile, pink and white dogwood blossoms.

Gemma finished her coffee and set the thermos down on the deck. She put her head back and closed her eyes.

*   *   *

When she woke up, the sun was halfway up the sky. Never before had she fallen asleep on the deck.

Empty thermos in hand, she carefully made her way to the steps Caleb had built for her so very long ago. Feeling unsteady, she eyed the railing, which she never, ever used, and then slowly started down.

The house was silent, the coffeemaker turned off, the cup she'd left for Logan gone. She found him sitting on the sofa, in a moss-green Izod polo, with the scrapbook open in his lap.

"Hungry?" she said.

He looked up. "I want, so very badly, to see her in person."

"We'll figure it out," she said.

"Soon," he said.

"All right. But I want to tell her first. In my own way."

"Of course. That's only fair. But when?"

"I think she'll be here, for a week or so, in June, after her exams are over."

"Not till June?" Logan shook his head. "Can't you just call her up? Or email her?"

"I want to tell her in person. And then break the news to Noreen. My other daughter, Laurel's older sister. She'll need to know, too."

Logan took a breath, let it out. "'Oh the tangled web we weave.'"

Gemma felt a chill.

For breakfast, she made French toast, which Logan ate in silence. He didn't mention their daughter, didn't ask what she'd been like as a child, who she might be turning out to be. Didn't suggest what he might like to see in the town where his beloved grandfather had gone to college.

"Is there more maple syrup?" was all he said, lifting the empty bottle as if toasting her.

Gemma shook her head. "What about powdered sugar?"

"Yes! That's exactly how my grandmother served French toast. With butter and powdered sugar."

Later, while rinsing their dishes in the sink, she asked how they should spend the rest of the day.

"Up to you," he said. "Where's your favorite place?"

"The mountains. You can *see* the Blue Ridge from here in Lexington, but you're not really *in* them. Shenandoah is farther away."

"How long would it take to be *in* them?"

"Maybe twenty minutes to the Blue Ridge Parkway, if we go through Buena Vista. About two and a half hours to Shenandoah National Park."

"Bway-na Veesta, you mean?" he said. "Spanish for 'beautiful view'?"

She turned around. "Here in Virginia, it's pronounced exactly the way I said it. Bew-nah Vis-tuh. Ask anyone. One explanation is that a family of Mexicans settled there, back in the 1800s, and they were too polite to correct their neighbors' pronunciation."

"No one else spoke Spanish, you mean."

"Why would they?" she said. "Most of the other settlers were Scottish. The Southern Appalachians, or so I've been told, reminded the Scots of their mountains back home."

"The very first settlers were here long before that."

"The Indians, yes. Well, they didn't speak Spanish, either."

Worried they were arguing, Gemma was relieved to see him smile.

"I don't mind a longer drive," he said. "Whichever you'd prefer."

"The place I loved the most in the Shenandoah National Park now makes me sad. As for the Blue Ridge Parkway, there are huge trees on either side of the road. You know the mountains are there, but you can drive for miles and miles without seeing them."

"Then what about your second favorite place?"

"The Skyline Drive itself, I guess." She shrugged. "It's worth the trip, for sure. Further south, though, the mountain laurel might be starting to bloom. The laurel I told you about, all those many years ago. The laurel that's not the tree your cottage is named after."

"I'd like to see any kind of laurel." He stood up. "Preferably the human you gave birth to."

He opened his arms, and she walked into them. "First, we need to figure out what to tell her." She took a step back. "Laurel has a built-in lie detector. Whatever we tell her has to be the absolute truth."

He sat down at the table again. "I was so depressed. A lot of that summer I barely remember at all."

"So there might have been other women you picked up on the beach?"

"There were not."

"Let's head south," she said. "And hope for laurel."

As they approached Buena Vista, Gemma didn't mention that Tim had grown up there. Didn't tell Logan about the terrible flooding that had driven her mother-in-law from the home she loved. That was in the past. Now it was beginning to look like it might be some sort of future.

Once they were on the Parkway, she explained that it

was a national park linking two larger parks, Shenandoah and the Great Smokies.

"Oh," Logan said. "I've always wanted to see the Smokies."

"Another day," she said. "But be on the lookout for shrubs with flowers like tiny white bowls. That's mountain laurel."

At the first overlook, Logan stopped the car and got out. While he was admiring the mountains, Gemma wandered down a faint path. And there, as if it had every right to exist, was a hemlock. A seemingly healthy one, maybe ten feet tall, its needles showing no signs of the wooly adelgid, at least none that she could see.

Soon Logan was standing beside her, asking what was wrong, why the tears?

"These mountains mean as much to me as Big Sur does to you," she said.

"They're beautiful, yes."

"To me, they're home. You know?"

"Sort of," Logan said. "Not really. Maybe I've had too many homes."

"And the hemlocks, most of them anyway, are dying. Or already dead. I wrote an article about them for the *Washington Post*."

"Gemma Sommerset," Logan said. "Travel Writer. So what have you written lately?"

"Zilch," she said. "Absolutely *nada*."

Back in the car, heading south again, Gemma consulted her map. "Ready for sandwiches? We can stop at the next overlook, if you'd like."

"What about here?" Logan activated the blinker, slowed down. "I'm hungry. Aren't you?"

"Federal law," she warned. "Stopping is permitted only at an overlook."

Logan sighed, sped up. "What if a kid gets carsick?"

"Don't know. Maybe that would be considered a federal emergency."

A few miles later, she cried out. "Stop, stop! Now! Right here!"

Logan pulled over and stopped. Gemma was out of the car before he'd turned off the engine.

"Just sitting here waiting for us." She pointed to an explosion of little pink flowers.

"Logan, meet mountain laurel. Laurel, this is Logan."

Logan took out his phone and began taking photos. He was motioning for Gemma to be included in one, when a white car suddenly braked to a stop behind his rental.

"The fuzz," Gemma said. "Uh oh."

A park ranger dressed in khaki walked up to them. "Good afternoon," she said. "Ranger Muriel here. Need to ask you to get back on the road. You can't park here, not even for laurel, which, I agree, is beautiful to the point of being downright sacred. But rules are rules. Always have been and always will be."

"We understand," Logan said. "Our daughter's name is Laurel. We saw the blossoms and couldn't resist."

"Where is she? Your Laurel?"

"Philadelphia." Gemma and Logan said this in unison.

"Pennsylvania?"

Logan flashed his smile. "The City of Brotherly Love, yes. Before we get back on the road, could I ask a favor?" He handed her his phone. "A photo of us and the laurel, one good enough to send to our Laurel?"

"Can't see the harm in that."

Once they'd decided where to stand, Ranger Muriel stepped back and took their photo. And a second one. She then returned Logan's phone to him, watched them get back in their car, and waved goodbye as they drove off.

Seated at a picnic table with a view of the hazy blue mountains, Gemma handed Logan a sandwich.

"I need to figure out what to tell them," she said.

"Who?" Logan said.

"My daughters. How do I say it? *I've been lying to you for years.*"

"Will you tell them at the same time?"

"That might be easier." She shrugged. "Or not."

Logan seemed to be thinking this over. "And then I can meet Laurel?"

"When she's ready."

He shook his head. "But how will you know?"

Another shrug. "We need my mother, to plot this all out."

"She wrote mysteries?" Logan said.

"She calculated probabilities."

"As in, Laurel might hate me?"

"I think," Gemma said, "it's far more likely that she'll hate me."

That night, in the master bedroom in Lexington, Gemma and Logan slept together. They then fell asleep.

In the morning, they slept together again.

"Not too bad for old folks," Logan said.

"What if I hadn't answered the phone when you called?" she said.

"Oh, but I'm so very glad you did!"

28

In June, before flying off to New Mexico to assist with an archeological dig near Taos, Laurel spent four days in Lexington. Gemma had invited Noreen to come, too, but since it was the end of the school year, Noreen felt she couldn't leave.

Laurel was so excited to have been chosen for the dig, hoping it would help her get into graduate school, that Gemma put off telling her about Logan.

But on the evening of the second day, during dinner, she pushed her plate aside. Took a deep breath. At the same table where she'd told Tim about Logan, she once again confessed.

The first time, meat loaf and mashed potatoes. For Laurel, chicken salad and sliced tomatoes. Cornbread muffins. Little green gherkins in a blue bowl. A bottle of pinot grigio.

"There's something I've been wanting to tell you,"

Gemma began.

Laurel looked up, raised her eyebrows.

"I'm sort of seeing someone."

"That's terrific, Mom."

"Honey, there's more." Gemma began shredding the paper napkin in her lap.

"Uh oh. You never call me honey."

"His name is Logan. Logan Rhodes. I met him twenty years ago. In California. I'd gone to Carmel to write an article about the town."

"And you kept in touch?" Laurel raised her eyebrows.

"That's the thing. We didn't. Stay in touch. He just showed up again. Out of the blue."

"I'm happy for you. Really, I am."

"The thing is." Although Gemma had been rehearsing this part for weeks, her mind had gone completely blank. What came out of her mouth was not at all what she had planned, so very carefully, to say. "You have two fathers."

"Will have, you mean."

"No, what I mean is. Or yes, in a way. Tim, who loved you very much, and Logan, who didn't even know about you but now that he does will love you, too."

"Plus, Noreen, I assume."

"What I'm trying so very hard to say is . . ." Gemma

took a deep breath, let it out. "Logan is your father. You are his child. His biological child."

Laurel shook her head.

"We had a fling, in Carmel. I thought I was too old to get pregnant, but somehow, I did."

Laurel drained her wine glass, went to the refrigerator, refilled the glass, and set the bottle on the table.

"I know what a shock this must be," Gemma said.

"You can't possibly. Because it's *not* a shock. Not really. This explains *everything*."

Gemma was mystified. "What are you talking about?"

"I knew I didn't belong. I thought maybe I'd been adopted, but Noreen told me, again and again, about the night I was born, in Charlottesville, and even though I wanted to believe her, I never really felt like I was truly part of this family. I didn't fit in. It's why I spent so much time at my friends' houses."

"How could you possibly have thought that?"

"Well, maybe because, as it turns out, it was true." Laurel picked up a cornbread muffin and glared at it.

"But you were loved. Tim knew you weren't his, but he wanted you. He loved you."

"Yeah, I know. It was just this weird feeling I had. Now I know why." She bit into the muffin.

"I wish you'd said something," Gemma said.

Laurel swallowed. Washed the cornbread down with more wine. "Would you have told me the truth if I had?"

"Honestly, I don't know."

"I'm going for a walk." Laurel pushed back her chair and left the kitchen. Slammed the front door behind her. When she returned, an hour later, she clomped up the stairs to her room.

Later that evening, Gemma was sitting on the sofa, staring into the stone-cold fireplace—wondering what to do next, what to say, whom to say it to—when Laurel, in a leopard-skin-patterned nightshirt, came downstairs, plopped down beside her, and demanded to be told the "whole damn story."

Gemma reached over to touch the silky material. "Love this. Where'd you find it?"

"Helen's mother gave it to her, but she didn't much like it, and I did, so she gave it to me."

"Your roommate, right?"

"Helen, yes. Now, tell me what the hell is going on."

"First, let me point out that your father—Tim, I mean—reacted in much the same way when I told him. He slammed the car door and went for a long walk."

"And your point is?"

"He came back and decided to stay. Because he wanted you, Laurel. He loved you. You did belong here."

After an exaggerated sigh, Laurel said, "So tell me about my other father."

Gemma began with the Carmel Library. Then the dog on the beach.

"A Dalmatian, if you can believe it."

"Named?" Laurel said.

"Gorgeous."

"Terrible name for a dog. Go on."

Gemma related every G-rated detail she could remember. She even mentioned the photo of Maggie, explaining that Maggie had died of leukemia, and Logan and his wife were grieving, and that's why they were living apart.

"I guess you're going to keep seeing him no matter what I think."

"What *do* you think?"

"I can understand why you and Dad lied to me. At least I think I can. But the fact is, you did. Lie to me." Laurel took a breath. "I don't think I can ever forgive you for that."

"And if Logan hadn't looked me up again, I'd still be lying. But he did look me up. And we realized we still care about each other."

"Oh, spare me. It's like some stupid romance novel."

Gemma didn't bother to reply.

"So, this Lowell fellow never knew about me?"

"Logan. He'd dumped me, so no, I didn't tell him. Your father . . . Tim and I had talked about breaking the news to you when you turned sixteen, but by then he was gone, and I just couldn't see the point."

"Dad knew I wasn't his?"

Gemma nodded. "He'd always wanted more children. You were like a gift."

"I don't believe you."

"Believe what you want," Gemma said. "What I'm telling you is true."

"I guess Noreen isn't really my sister, either."

"Of course she's your sister. If it hadn't been for her, you might've been born somewhere between Monticello and Lexington."

"Total non sequitur, Mom. Does she know?"

"Not yet, no." Gemma reached over and patted her daughter's arm.

Laurel pulled away. The two of them sat staring into the fireplace.

"Tell me about New Mexico," Gemma said. "What will you do there, exactly?"

"Dig."

Gemma waited.

"Uncover hidden secrets," Laurel said. "Buried so long by now that no one will be hurt by them."

And Gemma began to cry. Silently, at first, then audible sobs. Laurel turned to stare at her, then went into the bathroom, returned with a roll of toilet paper, and sat down again.

Gemma blew her nose. "He wants very much to meet you."

"So that I can take the place of his daughter who died?"

"Laurel, please."

"Don't tell me you understand how I feel. You can't possibly."

"All right. But consider this. If *you* should learn, when you're in your sixties, that you have a daughter you hadn't even known about, wouldn't you want to meet her?"

"Maybe. I might want to know first about that extended coma I must've been in."

Logan's wryly logical daughter, with—finally—a hint of her father's smile.

"You don't have to decide now," Gemma said. "I don't even know when I'll see him again."

A long silence from Laurel.

"Here's what I think," she said then, staring straight

ahead. "If he's old, and you still have feelings for him, then you'd better hurry the hell up."

With only a few hours' sleep, Gemma was in the kitchen, brewing coffee, at five-thirty. She then took the thermos up to the deck and sat down to wait for sunrise.

Next thing she knew, someone was squeezing her arm. "Mom. Wake up. Mom. Please. Open your eyes."

"I'm fine," Gemma said. "I dozed off, that's all."

"I saw you out here and knocked on the window, and when you didn't move, I got worried."

"I slept through sunrise?"

"The railing by the steps is loose," Laurel said. "You should get it fixed."

"I know, I know." Gemma opened the thermos, took a sip. "Want to sit down?" She moved her feet to make room.

"I'm fine." Laurel began pacing back and forth.

"Did you sleep?"

"Some. I kept thinking of things. Like, did my grandparents know?"

"Tim and I didn't tell a soul. No one guessed or even suspected."

Laurel stopped pacing. "*I* knew."

"I wish you'd said something."

"I was a kid. I didn't know what to say. I just felt so out of place."

"I sometimes felt that way myself, as a child," Gemma said.

"I felt that way *all the time.*"

"Well, maybe now you can stop."

Laurel resumed pacing. "I miss Dolly. I miss her so much."

"So do I. Our evening walks, especially."

"Dolly was the only one in the whole family who understood me."

Gemma let it go. "Let's walk down to Woods Creek later on," she said. "Pay our respects."

Laurel came to a sudden halt and stood frowning down at Gemma. "Why isn't there a door up here? A door would be so much safer for you than those steps."

"Tim didn't want a door. He was worried some Romeo would come courting and Noreen would let him in."

"You're making that up," Laurel said.

Gemma switched the thermos to her left hand, held up her right. "I'm not, I swear. The man who built this deck lives down in Bristol now. Caleb the Carpenter. Pretty sure he'd remember me, so why don't you call him up and ask him?"

29

Father and daughter met, in July of 2011, at the historic Sagebrush Inn in Taos, New Mexico. Built in the early 1930s (the travel writer learned), the original adobe structure, with thirteen guest rooms, had expanded to more than ten times that size. Georgia O'Keefe and Ansel Adams had stayed at the Sagebrush, as well as many movie stars. The lovely purple flowers blooming beside the parking areas were Russian sage.

It had been Laurel's idea for Gemma and Logan to stay at the Sagebrush, since her "dorm" was only a few miles away. But instead of accepting their offer to pick her up, she'd borrowed a friend's car for the momentous meeting.

"She's nervous, too," Logan said. "Wants to be able to make her escape, should she decide to cut and run."

At Laurel's urging, Gemma had invited Noreen to come to Taos, too. But it turned out to be the same week the Shepherds always spent in Virginia Beach. Noreen refused to leave Marshall alone with the kids.

He needed a vacation, and so did she.

On and on she went. Still angry, it seemed. About Logan, yes, but also the way Gemma had broken the news to her.

"You're calling to say you've been lying to Laurel and me all this time?" Noreen had said after a long silence. "And you're telling me by phone, when Laurel was able to hear it in person?"

"I'd asked you to come to Lexington while she was here," Gemma reminded her. "You said you were too busy."

"You didn't tell me *why* I should come. Not even a hint."

"Then I'm truly sorry, Noreen. What's most important here is that your sister needs your support."

"Well, she has it, but I'm not sure you ever will."

And Noreen had hung up.

As planned, Gemma and Logan were standing by the front entrance to the Sagebrush when Laurel arrived. She was wearing a royal blue tee and her good luck charm—the jade necklace Noreen had given her years before.

Since there was no need for introductions, Gemma stepped back. What she witnessed was mutual recognition. Father and daughter knew each other, even before they smiled.

Logan offered Laurel his hand, and she shook it.

"Hungry?" he said softly, and she nodded.

In the hotel restaurant, a waiter close to Laurel's age took their orders. After he left, no one knew quite what to say.

Logan came to the rescue by asking Laurel about her dig. Without making eye contact with either one of her parents, she described the Picuris Pueblo, south of Taos, which dated back to the eleventh century.

"So we're learning about a civilization based on what was left behind," she said.

"Like what?" Logan said.

"Everything from pottery to poop. More pottery than poop at Picuris, thank goodness."

"There may be a p-p-p-poem there," Logan said.

"P-p-p-possibly." And Laurel smiled. "In the Tiwa language, Picuris means 'people who paint.' They were pottery painters."

When their dinners arrived, another silence descended. This time it was Laurel who broke it.

"I don't know what to call you," she said to Logan.

"Whatever you feel comfortable with," Logan said.

"It's entirely up to you."

"Honestly? I'm not feeling comfortable with any of this."

Logan smiled. Laurel's own smile. "It may take some getting used to. For both of us."

"I guess Rome wasn't built in a day," Laurel said with a shrug.

"Nothing ventured, nothing gained," Logan countered.

"Haste makes waste," Laurel shot back.

"No time like the present."

"No fool like an old fool."

"Laurel!" Gemma poured herself more wine.

But Logan was smiling. "What you see is what you get."

"Look before you leap," Laurel replied.

"Never say never."

"Enough of this, you two," Gemma said. "We have all the time in the world."

"*Time-worn cliché!*" Logan said. "Ding, ding. Five-point penalty."

And they laughed, all three of them.

But after they'd ordered dessert, things went quickly downhill.

"I've been thinking," Logan said to Laurel. "If your mother and I got married here, in Taos, then you could come to the wedding. I've already looked into getting a marriage license. In New Mexico, it's surprisingly easy."

"Do I have a say here?" Gemma swallowed more wine, then set her glass down hard. "Why is it that no one ever even *thinks* about asking me?"

"The final one." Logan raised his glass to her. "The very final say is yours."

"Well then, thanks but no thanks." She emptied her wine glass. "I wasn't especially eager to get married the first time, when Tim never asked me, and now you haven't, either. You just assumed. Not every woman wants to be married, or feels a need to be married. If only we could go back to the good old days!"

"Mom," Laurel said. "Marriage has been around since the Paleolithic Era."

"So, you think we should get married?"

"What I think is, I'm outta here." Laurel stood up, brandished the car keys. "I'm off. You two need to figure this out. It is not my problem."

"Laurel," Logan said softly. "Please sit down."

Laurel sat.

"Gemma," Logan said. "I am so very sorry. Sometimes I get ahead of myself. We don't have to get married. Not now, not ever. Surely there were cavemen who stayed single." He took a breath. "Not to mention cavewomen."

Their waiter was dimming the lights. He gave Logan the check, and said the restaurant was closing.

"OK if we sit here for a while?" Logan said.

The waiter shrugged. "Fine by me. The manager may have other ideas."

"More wine?" Logan emptied the bottle into Gemma's glass.

Gemma glared at him. "Wine won't change my mind."

Laurel took Gemma's glass. "She's had way too much already. Anyway, we should probably leave. The manager's glaring at us."

Logan touched Gemma's arm. "Let's continue this conversation in our room."

Gemma shook her head. "You go on. I'd like to talk to Laurel alone. If that's all right."

Behind the hotel, prairie dogs were darting in and out of their holes in the sand, snapping to attention at the slightest sound. The sky was on fire.

"Look!" Laurel pointed to a weathered wooden cross. "A grave. It's old, but *someone* still remembers. See the trinkets?"

"Rodents and ancient graves," Gemma said. "So

here we are, then."

"Take a deep breath, Mom. I know this must be a little weird for you, too."

"Would it help if I married him?"

"Help what?" Laurel said.

"Make it less weird for you."

"Maybe. I don't know. Not really. Anyway, that's entirely up to you."

"The sunsets here are spectacular," Gemma said. "Have you noticed?"

"Every night. So, what did you want to talk to me about?"

"Anything," Gemma said. "Ask me anything."

"But I just met him. I don't know what to ask."

"Do you think you can ever think of him as your father?"

"I don't understand. He *is* my father, right? And so was Dad." Laurel took a deep breath, let it out. "I don't know what to call him. I think I'd feel a little better about all this if I did."

"His friends call him Low."

"As in Lo and behold?"

"L-o-w. Low Rhodes. Get it? As opposed to taking the high road."

Laurel nodded. "Exhibit A: Taking the low road, he blithely assumed you'd want to marry him."

"Yeah," Gemma said. "I was *not* expecting that."

A dismissive shrug from Laurel. "Maybe he was just nervous tonight. He's probably never met a daughter he didn't know he had."

"Laurel?" Gemma was close to tears.

"Yes, Mom?"

"How did you get to be so very, very wise?"

Part V

The Ceremony

30

Within days, Laurel had found a tribal elder named Luke who performed wedding ceremonies in the Taos dialect of the ancient Tiwa language. The marriage would be legal if they already had a valid marriage license.

Logan spent some time trying to explain why—for Gemma's sake as well as Laurel's—the marriage should be demonstrably legal. If anything were to happen to him, then he wanted his wife and daughter to inherit his estate.

"Can't you just change your will?" Gemma said. "Or not. I'm no gold digger."

Without a marriage license, Logan insisted, the ceremony would be meaningless.

"Not to me," Gemma said.

But she could not, even unofficially, marry the father of her younger daughter without letting her older daughter know. And the only way to do that was by phone.

"I'm in New Mexico, in Taos," Gemma began when Noreen finally answered.

"I know," Noreen said. "And we're in Virginia Beach."

"Having fun?" Gemma said.

"A blast. Are you?"

"It's beautiful here. I wish you'd been able to come."

"Has Laurel met him yet?"

"A few days ago, yes." Gemma stepped off the sidewalk and headed for a lawn chair in one of the grassy courtyards at the Sagebrush. "And I have some news. Looks like I'm getting married, sort of, on Sunday. Two days from now."

"Sort of?"

"You're invited, your whole family is. We could pick you up in Albuquerque tomorrow." Gemma sat back in the chair, stared up through pine needles at the very blue sky. "Laurel has arranged for a ceremony. She knows someone who knows someone who knows a tribal chief."

"Have both of you totally flipped?"

"You don't have to come, Noreen. I just thought you'd like to know."

"Well thanks, but we can't possibly leave on such short notice."

"I understand," Gemma said.

"Congratulations, Mom."

And Noreen hung up.

The next morning, Logan woke Gemma with a kiss on the back of her neck. "Hey you," he said. "For a tribal ceremony, in a language we don't understand, will there be rings?"

"Rings?" She turned to face him.

"Wedding rings," he said. "I have this sudden urge to buy you a ring. A non-wedding ring. Would that be all right?"

"Not necessary."

"But you might consider it?"

She shook her head, then kissed him, knowing what it might lead to, and it did.

After having lunch in town, they walked over to the Taos Plaza. It seemed a bit touristy, but then they were, of course, tourists. In one of the shops, they tried on sombreros, checked out the T-shirts and leather belts.

A beaded ring caught Gemma's eye. Blue, orange, and yellow—the colors of sunrise. She tried it on.

"Thought you didn't want a ring," Logan said.

"It's not a wedding ring, only a fun ring, except that

it's too big." She returned it to its wooden peg.

In a quiet corner at the back of the plaza was a shop that didn't seem to be trying to attract attention to itself. Logan opened the door and nodded to Gemma to precede him.

Seemingly alone in the store, they admired carved leather wallets, Navajo rugs, and paintings by local artists. As Gemma was trying on a colorful suede vest, a well-dressed man appeared. In the soft but urgent voice of a movie narrator, he encouraged them to look around. He then drifted away, toward the back of the store, where he took something from a glass display case. Having set whatever it was on top of the case, he mysteriously vanished.

"Guess we don't look like shoplifters," Gemma said, returning the vest to its hanger.

"He may be watching us through a peephole, ready to set off an alarm that locks the door. Wonder what he'd do if I kissed you?"

"Let's not find out."

Pretending to be dejected, Logan headed toward the back of the store. After leaning over the display case, he straightened up, then bent forward again.

"Gemma!" he sang out. "Gemma, come look."

What she found there gave her chills. A display of rings, against green velvet.

"How did he know?" Logan said softly. "How could he tell?"

He picked up a man's silver ring, etched with curlicues. "Ocean waves? All the way up here in the high desert?"

"Try it on," Gemma urged.

But the ring was too small for him.

A silver band inlaid with triangles of turquoise and lapis lazuli—a sky-meets-mountains pattern—caught her eye. It fit her perfectly.

"The Blue Ridge!" she whispered, extending her hand.

The ghostly owner appeared, with a ring similar to the one Logan had chosen, and then, without a word, left them alone again. The new ring was a perfect fit.

"But do you like it?" Gemma whispered.

"The waves have foam." Logan pointed. "A hint of foam, anyway."

Gemma didn't see any foam.

Again, the man materialized, his face a mask.

"We'll take these two." Without even asking the cost, Logan took out a credit card.

"You pay for mine, I'll pay for yours," Gemma insisted.

After the owner had left with their credit cards, they positioned their left hands next to each other on top of the glass case.

"Pacific Ocean meets Blue Ridge Mountains." Gemma said this softly, in the quiet store, where they were still the only customers.

"A geographic impossibility," Logan said.

"I'm not talking geography."

A mix-up in returning their credit cards reminded her that his full name was Logan J. Rhodes. The J., he explained with a grimace, was for Joaquín.

"A family name?" she said.

"Oh, let's not get into that now."

"Speaking of names," Gemma said. "You've been Logan Rhodes your entire life. Women are supposed to change their names when they get married. If you wouldn't mind, I'd really like to be Gemma Sommerset again. She had dreams. A year or two in Paris. If she'd gone, she might still be there, who knows? But she'd been sent to college to find a husband, so that's what she did."

"I don't care what you call yourself." Logan smiled. "Just don't call me late for dinner."

The Tiwa ceremony uniting Logan Joaquín Rhodes and Gemma Sommerset took place at the Sagebrush Inn on Saturday, July 23, 2011. With a late afternoon thunderstorm threatening to drench the tiled patio, the ceremony was moved inside to the bar.

The attendees included a group of Laurel's friends from the dig, along with a few guests and staff at the Sagebrush.

Gemma barely remembered her first wedding. This one, she felt certain, would be impossible to forget.

The bride did not wear white. The groom lacked a tie. Gemma was in moss-green jeans, Logan khaki slacks.

As Luke's oration came to an end, he gave the happy couple a solemn nod. Logan went first. "With this ring, I thee wed." Gemma echoed him, slipping the shiny new ring onto Logan's finger.

At that very moment, a double rainbow became visible outside. "Included in the ceremony," Luke whispered. "My own personal blessing."

31

On Sunday afternoon, the day after the wedding, Laurel took the newlyweds to visit La Hacienda de Los Martinez.

"Best wedding present I could think of," she said, insisting on paying their admission fees. "Think Stonewall Jackson House. The hacienda was built at about the same time."

"But with adobe, not brick," Gemma said.

"Very observant, Mom!"

"Tell us more," Logan said.

"The Martinez ranch was at the northern end of the Camino Real, a trade route extending all the way from Taos to Mexico City. This was a very busy place back then."

The hacienda consisted of two large courtyards surrounded by mostly windowless rooms, not all of which were open to the public. Gemma was fascinated by the high-ceilinged kitchen, with its corner fireplace and cast-iron pots and pans. Ladders led up to what a sign explained were beds where the servants could keep warm at night.

Other rooms held display cases for clothing and tools. One was filled with various kinds of looms. In another, Laurel stopped in front of two black wall plaques describing "The Slave Trade in New Mexico."

"I always thought it was just the South," she said. "I was so surprised to see this. I mean, I knew the Spanish had brought African slaves to Florida, back in the 1500s, but I had no idea they'd enslaved the Indians out here. Women and children, mostly."

"Slavery has existed since ancient times," Logan said quietly. "Egypt, Greece, Mesopotamia, you name it."

"That doesn't make it *right*," Laurel snapped. "We stole the Indians' land from them, and so did the Spanish. This was *their* country. They'd been here for thousands of years and were doing just fine without us. We call them Indians because Columbus thought he'd reached the Indies, when he was nowhere near. Or Native Americans, because of Amerigo Vespucci."

"In California," Logan said, "the Spanish priests tried to turn the natives into Catholics."

"Same here." Laurel nodded. "Have you been to the Taos Pueblo? Built *centuries* before Columbus even thought about sailing the ocean blue. The newest building there is the Catholic church."

That night, after brushing her teeth, Gemma found Logan slumped on the edge of the bed, staring disconsolately into the mirror above the heavy oak dresser. Alarmed, she sat down beside him.

Without looking at her, he took her hand. "How can I win her over?"

"Laurel?"

He nodded.

"Laurel found someone to marry us. She invited her friends to our wedding. This afternoon, she took us to her favorite place in Taos. What else do you want her to do?"

"Why didn't she want to have dinner with us tonight?"

"Maybe she had homework. She's getting course credits for this dig. You and I, we're on vacation here. Laurel isn't."

"So you think she'll come around?"

"She already has, Logan. Open your eyes."

He leaned toward her, his eyes wide. "One more question?"

"Shoot."

"What do you have against marriage?"

"Not sure I can explain."

"Can you try? I won't divorce you. Not sure I could, even if I wanted to."

How to tell him that, when she was growing up, all she was *ever* supposed to do in life was get married. The crystal-clear message being that without a husband, she would be no one. A nobody. A failure.

As a teenager, she'd used makeup and mouthwash, worn stockings and padded bras, so as to make herself more attractive to boys. She'd been sent to college to attract a husband. Someone whose career she would support, helping to ensure his success in the world.

"It was supposed to be my one goal in life. Marriage. The be all and end all. As if I couldn't possibly manage by myself."

"Do you regret marrying Tim?"

"Not really," Gemma admitted.

"Did you love him?"

"Most of the time. What about your wife?"

"Did I marry her for her money, you mean?"

"I would never ask you that."

"I'm not sure how I'd answer if you did."

32

Her first morning back in Lexington, Gemma overslept. Then, thermos in hand, she climbed the sunlit steps to the deck and sat down in her chair. While sipping coffee, she stared at her turquoise and lapis ring, visible proof that the wedding in Taos had actually happened.

No one in Lexington knew yet, and she wasn't planning to send out announcements. Those on her Christmas-card list could wait till December to hear. This included her increasingly fragile and forgetful mother-in-law, who was still in Florida with Tim's sister.

The person she most wanted to tell was Fontana. Wherever she was, Fontana would understand *everything*. Gemma's reluctance to have a formal ceremony, as well as her delight in knowing that most of the wedding guests had been complete strangers who didn't understand Tiwa any better than the bride and groom did.

As for changing her name back to Gemma Sommerset, what was the hurry? Driver's license, Social

Security, the IRS, and who else? It all seemed like such a huge hassle.

So much was still up in the air. Once Logan had sold his wife's mansion in San Francisco, where would they live—Lexington or Carmel? If both, then how much time would they spend in each place? Who would decide this? Based on what?

She wondered how long it would have taken for her parents to accept Logan as their son-in-law. As Laurel's father.

For Nat, she didn't have to wonder. Nat would've been thrilled with a new brother-in-law. He and Logan would've hit it off from the git-go.

Having made her way carefully down the steps from the deck, she set the empty thermos on the kitchen counter and, out of habit, poured some cereal into a bowl. But instead of adding milk, she wandered upstairs.

To her bedroom (she now thought of it that way), where the box of letters her father had written home from Japan had been sitting on a shelf in the closet for years. With the ink fading, the thin paper growing ever more fragile, hadn't the time finally come for her to read them?

Having set the box down on the desk in Tim's office, she carefully opened it. Inside were white, stationery-sized envelopes addressed, in her father's spindly handwriting, to her mother, in Columbus, Ohio. Someone had arranged the envelopes in chronological order.

Seated in Tim's old chair, she opened the first letter, dated August 30, 1945. On a troop ship headed for Japan, her terribly seasick father complained about having been ordered to carry a gas mask and "go black-out."

Intrigued, Gemma traveled across the Pacific with Captain Sommerset, who was already feeling better when, from Lower Tokyo Bay, he caught a stunning glimpse of Mount Fuji in the distance. Sounding both excited and relieved, he described Yokohama as having "modern buildings, wide streets, street cars running, plenty of electric lights."

But instead of a lively city, he ended up billeted in a hangar beside a burned-out airfield. Sharing his disappointment, Gemma put the letters aside and went back downstairs. She was in the kitchen, adding milk to her cereal, when the doorbell rang.

Celeste Newman lived two blocks away. Her daughter Lilly had gone to elementary school with Noreen.

"Come on in, Celeste," Gemma said, because that was how neighbors were supposed to greet each other.

Celeste stepped into the living room. "Can't stay. On my way to the dentist." She took a breath, raised her eyebrows. "I hear congratulations might be in order."

Gemma wondered exactly how much Noreen had revealed to Lilly.

"Why thank you, Celeste."

"You're getting married soon?"

Realizing that Celeste could spread the word as well as anyone, Gemma held up her left hand. "Already happened, in New Mexico."

"What an absolutely stunning ring!" Celeste said. "When can we meet the lucky man?"

"Soon," Gemma lied. "He has business to attend to in California first."

"California, hey! So will you move there, or will he move here?"

"We're still figuring all that out. How's Lilly? Is she still in DC?"

Rolling her eyes, Celeste reported that Lilly was about to change jobs again. "Thank goodness she has Noreen nearby. Your Noreen has always been such a positive influence on my dear Lilly."

After Celeste had hurried off to the dentist, Gemma went straight to the phone. Not only did Noreen answer, but she also had time to talk. And to insist that of *course* she hadn't told Lilly, or anyone else, including her own family, about the secret wedding.

"It's no secret. There was a ceremony in Taos. You could've been there, if you'd wanted to come."

"And if you'd given me a little more notice, I would've been there."

"I didn't have much notice myself," Gemma said. "Everything happened so quickly."

"But you've known him for, what, twenty years?"

"Are you angry, Noreen? You sound angry."

"Not sure how I feel. Is he there with you?"

"Logan? He's in San Francisco. After he sells his house there, I may join him in Carmel."

"For how long?"

"I don't know. None of this is settled yet."

"But you're happy?"

At this, Gemma nearly burst into tears. She took a deep breath, asked how the kids were.

"Ready to go back to school," Noreen said. "Dreading going back to school. You remember."

"Once school starts, maybe you and I can meet for lunch. Talk this through. At one of our halfway points."

Noreen seemed to be thinking this over, perhaps considering whether she was willing to meet halfway.

"Edinburgh," she said finally. "I love telling people I'm having lunch with my mother in Edinburgh."

33

But before Noreen could find time for lunch, Logan had left San Francisco and returned to his cottage in Carmel. On a sunny afternoon in early November, at the same airport where, twenty years before, he'd so coldly told her good-bye, he seemed genuinely happy to see her.

Having stowed her suitcases in a silver Volvo, he drove her to the cottage where their fairy tale had begun. From the outside, the cottage looked the same. Yes, the laurel trees beside the front door seemed slightly taller, but that's what trees did: they grew.

"Apologies for the mess," Logan said once they were inside, where piles of boxes hid the fireplace. "I put most of my books in storage while I was renting the place out. I've been waiting for you to help me reshelve them in some sort of order."

"I'll try," she said. "Your shelves look forlorn."

Upstairs, their bed had a new spread on it—a wavy

pattern of blue and orange. There were fluffy new, mint-green towels.

In the second bedroom sat the same bunk beds with the same bare mattresses.

Dinner that night was warmed up spaghetti, just like the first time.

"Love the new bedspread," she said. "Reminds me of sunrise over the Blue Ridge."

"Or, possibly, sunset over the Pacific?" Logan said.

"Maybe," she said.

"Tell me about Laurel."

"She's back at Penn. So busy that I don't hear from her much, just an occasional email."

"That's what I get," Logan said. "Every now and then, an email. Short and sweet, as they say."

Gemma was both surprised and pleased. Good for Laurel, keeping in touch with her father.

"Do you think she'll go back to New Mexico next summer?" Logan said.

Gemma shook her head.

"Maybe she'll come here?"

"Maybe," Gemma said. "Anything's possible."

Occasionally, Logan went into town for breakfast, but most mornings they ate together, in their kitchen, drinking coffee brewed on a Cuisinart he'd brought down from San Francisco. This was where she asked him, one bright morning, if he'd ever wondered, all those years ago, why she'd come to Carmel.

He shrugged a shoulder. "I was just glad to have made your acquaintance."

"But then you sent me away."

"You already had plane tickets."

"I would've stayed," she said. "And you knew it."

"I did, yes. So clue me in. Why were you here?"

She told him about her idea for a series of articles on poets who'd written in log cabins. Starting with Robinson Jeffers, who, she'd quickly learned, had done his best work in a stone house.

"Tor House," Logan said. "We can visit if you'd like. It's not far from here."

"Too late now." She confessed that her visit to the Joaquin Miller cabin in DC had been similarly disappointing.

"Turned out Miller *did* write poetry in that cabin. But not in Rock Creek Park. The cabin had been moved there from its original location, on 16th Street, and re-assembled. I bumbled that one, too."

"So you just gave up?"

"On that idea, yeah. But I learned a valuable lesson: don't do sloppy research."

After Tim died, she'd begun reading books by travel writers and by writers who enjoyed traveling, all of whom (she couldn't help noticing) turned out to be men: Peter Matthiessen, Lawrence Durrell, Paul Theroux, Bruce Chatwin, Ian Frazier, John McPhee, Graham Greene. Wondering if there had been courageous women travelers as well, she'd discovered that indeed there were a few. Although their books were harder to find, she'd managed to get several through an interlibrary loan.

She told Logan how Freya Stark, traveling solo, had visited Arabia in the 1930s and Turkey in the 1950s. And how Dervla Murphy, packing a .25 revolver, had ridden a bicycle from Dunkirk to Delhi in 1965.

"Impressive," he said.

"All I ever managed to write about was forests within driving distance of my house."

"So where would you like to go?"

"Japan, maybe."

"Japan?" He frowned. "Why?"

"I'd like to try to visit the places where my father was stationed."

"But why?"

"Not sure I can explain it." That it would be a way of paying homage to a father she hadn't always appreciated wasn't the full story.

"Surely you've heard about the Fukushima disaster," Logan said. "Only a few months ago. People here are even worried about radioactive debris washing up on our beaches."

"I know," she said. "We'd have to wait till it's safe. In the meantime, maybe I'll try again to write about Carmel."

"Hasn't changed much." He shrugged.

"What if I interviewed you?" She made quotation marks with her fingers. "'The Man I Met on the Beach Who Asked Me to Organize His Library.'"

This elicited a smile. "What a fantastic pick-up line! Did he want to discuss Nabokov?"

She'd given Logan's phone number and mailing address to her daughters, although both preferred email. Noreen was the first to get in touch, asking if they planned to return to Virginia for Christmas, saying she was hoping they could all celebrate together in Fairfax, as usual.

Logan seemed as thrilled by the invitation as Gemma was. Said he hadn't really celebrated Christmas for years.

Still, Gemma couldn't help wondering: had Laurel

persuaded her sister to give Logan a chance? Or had Noreen somehow come to her senses on her own?

On Thanksgiving morning, Noreen called.

"Laurel sends greetings as well," she said. "She's gone off to a secluded mountain cabin with a new boyfriend."

"I had no idea," Gemma said. "Where?"

"Don't know. She was extremely vague about their plans."

"Do you know his name?"

"Roberto. From Peru. We may be able to meet him at Christmas."

"So, it's serious?"

"Sure sounds like it," Noreen said.

Logan claimed to be eager to meet Noreen. But Gemma knew. The person he most wanted to see was Laurel.

"What's Noreen like?" he asked one morning at breakfast.

"She's a lot like Tim's mother," Gemma said, "for whom she was named. It's downright eerie. They both love to cook. Noreen learned to read by following recipes her grandmother sent to her from Florida. I can promise you an excellent Christmas dinner."

"And Laurel?" he said. "What did she like to do as a child?"

"Visit cemeteries."

Logan's eyes went wide. "She did not get that from me."

"The cemetery near our house was where she took her first steps. So *very* proud of herself—I wish you could've been there."

"And if I'd only known, I would've," Logan said. "Been there. I would've found a way."

The day after Thanksgiving, they drove down to Big Sur. At Buzzards Roost, with the Pacific sparkling beneath them, Logan put his arm around her. And she burst into tears.

"Gemma, what's wrong?" he said in alarm.

"It's so beautiful."

"Then why the tears?"

She took a deep breath and attempted to explain the unexplainable.

"Such a very strange feeling." Another breath. "Never felt like this before. Or wait, maybe I have."

"Because of Big Sur?" he said. "The ocean?"

She shook her head. "It has less to do with *where* I am than *who* I am. Or who I seem to have become. Whom? The person I am now."

As a horseback-riding teenager, having soared over jumps on a trail near a mountain lake, she'd envisioned herself as being brave enough to accomplish just about anything.

But had she ever gone to Paris? Non.

Still, this older and wiser Gemma was perfectly content to be who she actually was, a sort-of-married (for the second time) mother of two very different daughters who'd grown up loving each other and still did. And she was thrilled to be exactly where she was, with Logan, looking out at the Pacific, when all her life she'd thought she could be happy only in the Blue Ridge.

"Do you know the Dixie Chicks song 'Loving Arms'?" she said.

"I don't even know the Dixie Chicks."

"Actually, I think 'Loving Arms' was written by Kris Kristofferson."

"Don't know him, either." Logan shrugged. "Should I?"

Gemma nodded. "Kris Kristofferson was a Rhodes Scholar. He studied William Blake at Oxford, then ended up in Nashville, writing country music. You have a daughter who grew up listening to country music. The Dixie Chicks version of 'Loving Arms' was one of Laurel's favorites. She would sing along while I was fixing dinner at night."

"Whose loving arms are they?"

"A man's, of course. The woman who'd once loved him has been alone for a very long time and is wishing they could get back together again."

Logan stared up at the sky.

"The really good love songs are wistful, don't you think?" Gemma said. "'Send in the Clowns.' 'Here's that Rainy Day.' 'Didn't We.'"

Logan seemed to be considering this. He turned to her. "Are we making our poem rhyme?"

She nodded.

And all because, years ago, on a Sunday afternoon, she'd decided to brave the multiple flights of steps down to Carmel Beach. Where a Dalmatian named Gorgeous had come up to her. And, because her father had liked Nabokov, she'd gotten into a conversation with Gorgeous's owner. Whom she'd then followed to his cottage. Where, against all odds, she'd become pregnant.

Twenty years later, on a Friday night in Lexington, Virginia, when she was almost asleep, she'd decided to answer the phone.

What were the chances of that particular series of events?

Minimal to none, her mother would've said.

Logan took her hand, led her back down the trail. Looking for a secluded spot for a picnic, he veered off into a grove of redwoods.

"Does this look like the place?" he said.

"A little. Maybe. It was so long ago."

"You think Laurel might have been conceived amongst the redwoods?"

"My money's on the beach in Carmel," Gemma said. "With the full moon looking on."

A faint trail ended at a redwood log sprouting ferns. Logan sat down on a section of bare bark. "This could become a nurse log, with baby redwoods taking root as it decays."

"A mama log?" Gemma looked around. "Rattlesnakes *love* logs."

"We'll have this one all to ourselves." He patted the bark beside him. "Or do you still worry about splinters?"

This made her laugh. "Your steps down to the beach. You remember that!" She sat down beside him and removed two turkey sandwiches from her backpack.

"I even remember how rude I was at the airport. I'd apologize, but . . ." Logan raised his hands, made quotation marks with his fingers. "'Men don't have to apologize.'"

"Who said that?"

"My father. At least I think he was my father. His name was Mike."

In Taos, he'd been reticent about revealing 'family stuff.' "Was this in Montana?"

"Idaho."

"What's Idaho like?"

"In the northern part, in summer, the streams are overflowing with Canadian snow melt. So cold it hurts to wade in. Hurts like hell to have to stand there for as long as someone tells you to, especially someone named Mike." He took a breath. "But mostly, I lived with my grandparents, in Montana."

"On a ranch." She handed him a sandwich, watched as he slowly unwrapped it and took a bite. "Do you ever go back?"

He shook his head. "It's a housing development now. Ranch houses where there used to be a ranch."

She changed the subject. "Do you think Laurel can visit us in Carmel?"

"Of course she can. I hope she will. Noreen, too, if she'd like." He gazed up at the redwoods. "Do you have siblings?"

"I did. My brother Nat. He disappeared in Vietnam."

"I'm so sorry."

"I miss him every day."

Logan took her hand. "Don't think I had any siblings. I have lots of cousins, though. My grandfather Rhodes had five boys and one girl."

"Never knew my grandmother," he went on. "She died giving birth to my mother."

"And your mother's name?" Gemma ventured.

"Catherine. After my grandmother. Last time I saw her, I was ten." Logan cleared his throat. "That's all for now."

34

In mid-December, they closed up the cottage in Carmel and flew to Virginia. It was their first time flying together, and by the time they finally arrived in Lynchburg, on a much-delayed flight from Charlotte, Gemma was thinking it might be their last.

At two a.m., with no cabs available at the Lynchburg airport, Gemma managed to find a motel willing to send a van to pick them up. The teenaged driver was as cheerful as Logan was sullen.

"Seat belts fastened?" he chirped, after stowing their suitcases in the back.

"Yep," Gemma said. She gave Logan a nudge, located the strap for him.

"So, where y'all from?" the driver asked as he pulled away from the curb.

"I was born here in Lynchburg," Gemma said. "Live in Lexington now."

"Where'd you go to high school?"

Logan cleared his throat. Loudly.

"Don't mean to be rude," Gemma said. "Do you

mind? We're a little too tired to chat right now."

"Don't mind at all. My dad was always telling me to button my lip."

At the motel, Logan stood glowering by the elevators while Gemma checked them in, charging the room to her credit card. He then shoved their suitcases into the elevator and waited for Gemma to push the button for their floor.

"Airport motels *always* suck," he snapped when she couldn't get the key card to work. But then it did work, and they were in a pleasant room with two queen-size beds.

"His and hers." She pointed at one of the beds. "This one's mine."

She'd brushed her teeth and was half asleep when she realized Logan was behind her, his voice in her ear. "Grandma, what nice thighs you have."

"Can't this wait till tomorrow?" she said.

"Wolves, my dear, are nocturnal."

"We're both tired," Gemma said. "And grumpy."

"Wrong fairy tale. Anyway, I thought Virginia was for lovers." He slipped a hand under her nightgown.

She was considering acquiescing, turning toward him, when she realized that the wolf, breathing heavily, had fallen asleep.

By the time they woke up, the motel's free breakfast was no longer available. No, the woman behind the counter told them, they couldn't pay for a bowl of cereal. Yes, she said, pointing to a coffee machine in the corner, they could have all the coffee they wanted. The closest restaurant? A pizza place, but it didn't open till noon.

While they were sipping coffee from paper cups, Gemma suggested that they take the motel's van to the airport, have breakfast there, then get a cab to Lexington.

Logan had a better idea. A taxi could pick them up at the motel, take them to a restaurant that was still serving breakfast, wait while they had pancakes or whatever, and then drive them to Lexington.

So that's what they did.

For the three months they'd been in Carmel, Gemma's friend Marie had been keeping an eye on the house. Still, it seemed so musty that Gemma immediately opened all the windows, upstairs and down.

"Didn't know it ever got this cold in Virginia," Logan grumbled.

"We have four seasons here," she said. "This one's called winter. Why don't you put on a sweater? I know you brought one."

"It'll take me a while to adapt, Gemma. It always does. Why don't you try to be patient?"

And he smiled. The smile he must have relied on, all his life, to calm troubled waters.

The smile Marie couldn't help noticing when she stopped by with a fried chicken dinner, along with cereal and milk and a loaf of bread.

"Marie's an artist," Gemma said, after introducing her to Logan. "The watercolors above the sofa are hers."

"I noticed those," Logan said. "How could I not? They're lovely. The Blue Ridge, right?"

"Yes!" Gemma and Marie said this in unison.

That's when Logan smiled.

Her eyes on Logan, Marie took a step back. Cocked her head. Started to say something, then decided not to.

"Thanks so much for the food," Gemma said. "And for taking such good care of the house. Can you stay for dinner?"

Marie shook her head. "Better get on home."

"Then let me walk you to your car." Because Marie was someone she could tell, the kind of friend who could—and would—keep a secret.

"How should we handle this?" Gemma said when

they were outside. "What should we say when someone notices?"

"That his smile is a lot like Laurel's?" Marie said. "Just shrug. Blame it on pure coincidence."

Gemma gave a tiny shrug. "Like this?"

Marie spoke softly. "I remember, years ago, when you were having trouble getting pregnant. So, a sperm bank? You searched for the donor?"

Gemma shook her head. "A beach in California. Under a full moon."

Marie's eyes widened. She blinked. "OK," she said. "Got it."

"Tim was angry at first. Of course he was. But he'd always wanted more children and came to see Laurel as a blessing."

"Then that's what you tell people," Marie said. "'Tim loved Laurel.' If anyone's ever rude enough to ask."

The next morning, eager to greet the sun, Gemma carefully slid out of bed and tiptoed downstairs. Having brewed enough coffee for two, she poured half of it into her thermos and climbed the steps to the deck.

Thrilled to be back in her chair, sipping from the familiar thermos, she heard the back door open. "Gemma?" Logan called. "Gemma? Are you out here?"

"On the deck," she called down to him. "Come join me."

"But it's pitch dark."

"Not for long." Dawn, in living color, was on its way. "There's a light switch. Inside, to the right of the back door."

The porch light came on. Then Logan, in his bathrobe, climbed the steps.

"Your railing's loose," he said.

"I don't use the railing."

"But what are you doing up here?"

"Waiting for sunrise."

"What an extraordinarily peculiar woman I married."

She moved her legs aside, invited him to sit down.

"No thanks. I'm going back to bed."

"But you'll miss it."

"As I usually do, Gemma. Lately we've been missing sunrise together."

She gave an audible sigh, as if sorry to see him go. Vowed never to admit to this man she loved that the most glorious sunrises were the ones she had all to herself.

A few days later, while they were walking along the

Woods Creek Trail, she told Logan about scattering Dolly's ashes in the creek.

"Laurel's love of Dalmatians was there from the beginning?" he said. "You never once encouraged it?"

"Cross my heart," Gemma said. "She was born with it."

"Not sure that's possible."

"Who knows what sorts of things we can inherit? My mother's mother didn't like pistachios. Neither do I."

"But Gorgeous was the only Dalmatian I ever had."

"And Gorgeous led you to me. And we had a child. Who has your smile and likes Dalmatians."

"That's not genetics, Gemma. It's the luck of the draw, as my grandfather liked to say."

"The grandfather who went to Washington and Lee?"

"He's the only one I had."

"This trail will take us there." Gemma pointed. "To the campus."

Logan came to a halt. He stood staring up into a maple tree clinging to the last of its red leaves. "Then Papa might've stood in this very spot. Never imagining that, years later, one of his great-granddaughters would live nearby." He turned to her, his eyes wide. "What are the chances of that!"

From the other side of the creek came crashing sounds. A deer, racing downhill, was soaring over any boulders or underbrush in her way. Perhaps the same doe Gemma had seen the summer Dolly died.

"Nearly everyone thinks Lexington has a deer problem," she said. "To me, though, they're dear friends."

"'A pun my word,' as my grandfather liked to say. And the deer? Do they feel the same way about you?"

She shrugged. "Maybe. They sure do spend a lot of time in my yard."

35

When visiting Noreen and her family in Fairfax, Gemma and Laurel usually shared a small room in the basement. For Christmas 2011, Gemma had reserved two rooms at a nearby Marriott.

Upon checking in, however, she learned that one of the reservations had been cancelled. She immediately called Noreen, who explained that Roberto had broken up with Laurel.

"She's not coming?" Gemma said.

"She's staying here with us, as usual," Noreen said. "Arriving tonight, on the train."

After hanging up, Gemma relayed the news to Logan. "They're sisters," she said. "They've always been close."

"Can we at least meet her train?" Logan said.

Gemma shook her head. "She'll take the Metro to Vienna."

Logan sank down on the bed. "You're speaking a foreign language."

"Driving into DC would be a bad idea. Laurel will

call Noreen when she gets in and then take the Metro to Vienna. Metro's like—what do you call it?—BART."

"Dangerous time of year, Christmas." Logan began picking at a loose thread on the red-and-gold bedspread. "Can we at least meet her in Vienna?" He looked up with a wry smile. "Assuming I'm not talking about Austria."

Noreen had a better idea. She would pick them up at their hotel and drive them to the Metro station.

"That's very kind of you," Gemma said.

"Maybe I'm just anxious to meet my new stepfather," Noreen said.

Which seemed to be the case. As soon they'd walked out of the hotel, Noreen, who'd been standing beside her car, hurried toward them.

"I'm Noreen," she said to Logan. "The other daughter."

At the Metro station, before driving off to search for a parking space, Noreen instructed them to wait outside. It wasn't long before Laurel came out, wearing the olive-green coat Gemma had given her the previous Christmas. Wrapped around her neck was the red-and-green-plaid wool scarf Tim's mother had ordered for her from Scotland. Noreen had a similar scarf, in a slightly different plaid.

Logan hurried to his daughter, gave her a hug, and

took her suitcase.

Gemma linked arms with her. "Noreen's saving dinner for you."

"Or we can stop somewhere along the way," Logan said. "Just say the word."

"The word is Amtrak hot dog," Laurel said. "I'm fine."

And she seemed fine. Dressed for the occasion in red and green. Not freaking out. Keeping it all bottled up inside.

When Gemma and Logan arrived at Noreen's the next morning, which was Christmas Eve, Marshall, Noreen's fastidious husband, greeted them at the door. He then went back to rearranging the ornaments his four children had already hung on the Christmas tree. The "re-decorator," Noreen called him.

Noreen and her daughters were busy in the kitchen. Gemma knew better than to offer to help. Christmas dinner would be served on Christmas Eve, with enough leftovers to get them through Christmas Day itself.

Laurel was in the basement with her nephews. Standing at the ping pong table in purple slippers and a pair of jeans, with her Scottish scarf peeking from a blue V-neck sweater, she looked up when her parents came down the basement steps.

"Oh, no," Gemma said in mock horror. "Not the puzzle again."

"S'posed to keep us busy down here," Frank, the thirteen-year-old, said.

"And look! We've already turned all the pieces right side up." Russell, the eldest, shaded his eyes. "And gone snow blind."

"All the pieces are white?" Logan said.

"Polar bears in the snow," Laurel said. "So, slightly different shades of white. A few black spots—eyes and noses."

"Gray toenails," Russell reminded her.

"Well," Logan said. "There must be a box with the picture on it."

"Mother hides it," Russell said. "Every year."

"She wants us to stay down here," Frank said. "Not bother her in the kitchen."

"Then should we try to find the corner pieces?" Logan said. "That would be a start."

"We don't bother," Laurel said. "We never, ever bother. Mostly, we just get the giggles."

And she demonstrated, laughing till she cried.

Gemma went to her daughter, put her arms around her. "Let's go upstairs."

"I need to put some shoes on first." Laurel hurried to her room and shut the door.

Noreen's kitchen reminded Gemma of Grandmother Noreen's kitchen in Buena Vista—pots on the stove, pans waiting to go into the oven once the turkey was done, measuring cups and measuring spoons and mixing bowls everywhere. The sink full of dirty dishes and implements. Delicious odors.

Noreen and her daughters, Katherine and Jessica, aged ten and eight, wore matching green aprons with red ties. Even the potholders were Christmassy.

"How can we help?" Laurel said.

"A quick trip to the grocery store?" Noreen said. "Easy to remember. SOS. Salt, orange juice, and sage. First time in my life I've *ever* run out of salt."

As if he and Noreen were in cahoots, Logan quickly handed over the car keys, said he'd rather sit and admire the tree.

"Nice car!" Laurel said, once she was buckled in. "Subaru Outback?"

"Yep. Logan drove off to Roanoke one afternoon, and this is what he came back in. Said I needed a new car."

"You did," Laurel said. "For years, now. Love the blue."

"Blue Subaru. Bet you can't say that three times in a row."

"That, that, that," Laurel said. "See, I'm fine."

Gemma turned into the giant parking lot and located a parking space.

"Before we go in," she said gently. "If you don't mind my asking. Five words or less: what happened with Roberto?"

"Not ready yet," Laurel said. "Still digesting. You wait here. I'll do the shopping." She opened the door, then pulled it shut again. "Got a Kleenex?"

"In the glove compartment."

"Still called that, isn't it?" She sniffled. "When was the last time you put gloves in the glove compartment?"

"Never ever did," Gemma said. "Not even once."

Laurel found a packet of Kleenex and blew her nose. "OK. Off to get SOS. ASAP."

Instead, she began to cry.

"He lied to me." She took a breath. "I have two fathers. Roberto has two girlfriends." Another breath. "Maybe more."

"I'm so sorry, honey. Where is he now?"

"Lima. With her. From her parents' balcony, you can see the Pacific." Laurel blew her nose. "He may be dropping out of school."

"Why would he do that?"

"He was caught cheating. I didn't know that, either."

"Want to give me the list?" Gemma said. "You stay here."

Laurel obliged. "Really love this blue," she said. "Like the mountains. Or a mood."

"Or a moon," Gemma said.

At dinner that night, Logan seemed uncomfortable. Worried about something.

"Laurel's scarf," he said, when they were back in their hotel room.

"It's Scottish. A gift from Tim's mother."

"And Laurel always wears it at Christmas?"

"Not always. Why?"

He sank down on a bed. "Bruises," he mumbled. "It's how my mother hid hers."

"You think Roberto may have tried to hurt her?"

"Could you maybe find out? If the scarf is covering something up, then we should know."

* * *

On Christmas Day, Laurel wore the scarf with a red sweater. After all the presents had been opened, she and Gemma gathered up the wrapping paper and took it to the pantry off the kitchen.

"I've always liked that scarf," Gemma said, stuffing paper into the recycling bin. "Cashmere?"

Laurel shrugged. "Pretty sure it's 100% Scottish wool."

"May I see the label?"

Without hesitation, Laurel removed the scarf and handed it over, exposing her unblemished, unbruised neck.

"You're right," Gemma handed it back. "Don't know why I thought it might be cashmere."

"Do you mind that I'm wearing it?"

"Why would I mind?"

"With Pops here, and all. I mean, it was Daddy's mother who gave it to me."

"Pops? Is that what you've decided to call him?"

"It's how he signs his emails. I don't know what to call him. This just feels so freakin' awkward."

"Is that why you're wearing the scarf?"

"Maybe. I don't know." Laurel quickly crumpled more wrapping paper. "Do you mind?"

"Not if it helps. Does it?"

"I don't know. I don't know anything. Can we just set all this paper on fire?"

Back at the Marriott, Gemma told Logan that Roberto had gone home to a girlfriend in Peru.

"Forever?"

"Who knows? And the scarf is just a scarf. I checked."

Logan's hand went to his neck. "Thank goodness."

December 26th, a Monday, was a federal holiday.

Logan wanted to drive into Washington. Not to see the White House or the Capitol or even the National Christmas Tree. His grandfather had once stayed at the Mayflower Hotel. The site Logan most wanted to see was the Mayflower's lobby.

Hoping Laurel would want to come with them, they drove over to Noreen's house. Where Laurel, who'd never even heard of the Mayflower Hotel, surprised them by saying she'd love to go.

Marshall didn't think the three of them knew the area well enough to try to drive in to DC. Nor should they take the Metro, which would be operating on a reduced schedule. So, Noreen offered to drive, reminding her husband that, with all the government offices and museums closed, the usually unbearable DC traffic wouldn't be so bad. She'd never been inside the Mayflower but knew exactly where it was. If Marshall didn't mind staying home with the kids.

"You deserve a day off," he said to her. "Don't mind at all."

After finding a parking space on 17th Street, Noreen led them west along DeSales Street. "Looks like we can get into the Mayflower from here," she said, pointing to a side door. "The main entrance is on Connecticut Avenue."

"Main entrance, please," Logan said, so they kept going.

"Magnificent!" he whispered, once they were inside, where stately Christmas trees, their lights aglow, lined the walls of the enormous lobby, and chandeliers hung from the ceiling. Reflecting the various forms of light, the polished marble floors added to the spectacle.

"Truly awesome," Laurel said. "I'm so glad we came."

"Are there hotels like this in Philadelphia?" Gemma asked her.

"Not that I know of," Laurel said. "I've heard that

Wanamaker's, the department store, used to be the place to go at Christmas. Still is, maybe, but it's a Macy's now."

"The Mayflower's a Marriott," Logan said.

"Noooo!" Noreen said. "I didn't know that."

"When was your grandfather here?" Gemma asked.

"During his time at Washington and Lee. So, sometime around 1910 or so?"

"A hundred years ago," Laurel said. "Imagine a tradition lasting that long!"

"Maybe you'll bring your children here someday," Logan said.

Laurel shrugged. "Not sure I'll ever have children."

After Logan had treated them to lunch, Noreen suggested walking up to DuPont Circle. Her summer job during college had been in that area.

"There could be a demonstration going on," she said.

"On the day after Christmas?" Gemma said.

"Why not?"

Logan begged off, preferring to watch what was going on at the Mayflower, but Gemma and Laurel followed Noreen north, along Connecticut Avenue, under cloudy skies.

While they were waiting to cross a side street, Gemma noticed a black-haired woman peering into the window of a clothing store. Exhibiting Fontana's excellent posture, the woman was holding the hands of two little girls with pigtails.

Could it be? Gemma thought. After all these years, Fontana and I will reconnect on Connecticut Avenue?

"Fontana!" she cried out. "Oh, Fontana!"

The woman didn't respond.

The light changed, and Gemma hurried across the street. "Fontana!" she called again. As best friends, they'd told each other their deepest secrets. That would continue. They had so much to catch up on.

Her heart hammering, Gemma approached the store. Perhaps reacting to a reflection in the window, the woman turned around.

Not Fontana. Not even close.

"I'm so sorry," Gemma said. "I thought you were an old friend."

"Surprised you have any," the woman said with a scowl.

Gemma backed away. Her daughters rescued her, guiding her along the sidewalk.

"Who's Fontana?" Laurel said softly.

"My very best friend from Lynchburg." On the verge of tears, Gemma took a deep breath. "Haven't seen her since my wedding day."

"Does she live here in Washington?" Laurel said.

"I don't know where she is," Gemma said. "Alaska, maybe, last I heard, but she could be anywhere."

At Dupont Circle, there were people sitting on the edge of the circular basin beneath an enormous white marble fountain, its water seemingly turned off for the winter. Pedestrians calmly strolled the park's sidewalks. On the day after Christmas, 2011, there were no signs of protest. Peace reigned.

"I've never seen it this quiet," Noreen said. "There was always *someone* here upset about *something*."

"In Philadelphia," Laurel said, "people protest at the Liberty Bell."

"What about that organization you worked for?" Gemma asked Noreen. "Did they ever demonstrate here?"

Noreen laughed. "By handing out free condoms, you mean?"

"But I thought it was all about the environment."

"It was," Noreen said. "There are way too many people on this planet. Millions more now than there were when I worked there. The goal was to convince couples to have only one or two children. Or no children at all."

Gemma and Laurel exchanged glances.

"I know, I know," Noreen said. "Shoot me."

"It's OK," Laurel said. "I don't want children, so between the two of us, we'll be fine."

"No, no, no." Noreen shook her head. "Children are *everything*. You'll see."

36

In June, when her exams were over, Laurel flew from Philadelphia to Carmel. The day before her arrival, Logan quietly made up the lower bunk in the second bedroom, while Gemma hung new, southwestern-themed towels in the small bath.

At the airport, while waiting for her suitcase, Laurel excitedly told them she might be staying at Penn for graduate school—*if* she could come up with a dissertation topic.

"Surely you don't have to decide that now," Gemma said. "You haven't even graduated."

"But I've taken some graduate courses," Laurel said. "I've been on a dig. So I should have a few ideas. And I do. I'm interested in the very earliest Americans."

"What about that tribe near Taos?" Logan said.

Laurel shook her head. "They've already been studied to death."

As they drove through town, with Logan acting like a tour guide, Laurel said very little. But once he'd parked in the garage and unlocked the front door of the cottage for which she'd been named, she perked up.

"Wow! Look at all these books!" Doing exactly that, she took a stroll around the shelves.

"Double wow!" she said after noticing the sliding glass door to the deck. "Is that the Pacific?" She gripped the door's handle. "Some of the very earliest Americans sailed across the Pacific, you know. Not everyone trekked down from Alaska."

She slid the door open, stepped out onto the patio. "Is there a beach?"

"At the bottom of the steps," Logan said. "But you have to be twenty-one."

"Ha, ha," Laurel said, and down she went.

"It's her very first ocean," Gemma said.

"Never seen an ocean? How can that be?"

"Tim went to accounting conventions. That was all the traveling he ever wanted to do. After he died, I thought about taking Laurel to Myrtle Beach, where my family had always gone, but ..."

Logan put an arm around her. "We do what we can. And somehow, things have a way of working out."

The next morning, Gemma found a note from Laurel on the kitchen counter. Sittin' on the sand somewhere, starin' out at the Pacific. Come find me.

And where was she? Very close to the spot where, years before, Gorgeous had found Gemma.

"Feel like coffee?" Gemma held up the thermos she'd just filled.

Laurel shook her head. "No thanks. I know you said I'd like it when I got older. But." She gave a shrug.

Gemma set the thermos on the sand. "If I sit down beside you, will you help me up when we're ready to leave?"

Laurel smiled. Her father's smile. "I'll sure try."

They sat in silence, Gemma sipping coffee, Laurel seemingly transfixed by the horizon.

"If we were to sail due west from here," she said, "where would we end up?"

"You're giving me goose bumps," Gemma said. "The very first time I set foot on this beach I wondered the very same thing."

"Does Pops have a world atlas in that amazing library of his?"

Gemma nodded. "Near the front door, with the oversized books."

"Google might help, but I'd rather sit with a map on my lap."

"Agreed," Gemma said. "More poetic that way. I told Logan the Pacific was your first ocean. Was I right about that?"

Laurel nodded. "I was supposed to go to the Jersey Shore one weekend. Didn't happen. Can't remember why."

Later that morning, with an old *Hammond World Atlas* open on her lap, Laurel determined that a boat sailing west from Carmel would run into Japan, not far from Tokyo.

"Your grandfather," Gemma said, "sailed to Japan from San Francisco, in August of 1945, and returned in April of the following year. He was terribly seasick, both going and coming."

"Just think how sick he would've been in an outrigger canoe, or a longboat, or whatever," Laurel said.

"So you think some very early inhabitants of Japan might've sailed all the way to California?"

Laurel shrugged. "The Polynesians got as far as Easter Island. Maybe even to what is now Chile, as well."

"I've always wanted to go to Chile," Gemma said. "It's got everything. Deserts, the Andes, Patagonia, Easter Island."

"Then do it! Pops will go with you. Where is he, anyway?"

"Not sure," Gemma said.

Minutes later, the front door opened, and in stepped an excited Dalmatian, with Logan gripping its leash.

"She has to be home by three," he said. "Her name's Maybellene. Belongs to a friend of mine."

Laurel leaned down and told Maybellene she was beautiful.

"I'm afraid she'd agree," Logan said. "Spoiled rotten, she is."

"Thank you, Pops. Can we take her down to the beach?"

"Do we want to eat lunch first?" Gemma said.

"Lunch?" Laurel and Logan objected in unison.

As soon as they'd returned to the cottage, Maybellene lay down beside the fireplace, as though she'd inherited that spot from Gorgeous, and fell asleep. Lunch was soup and sandwiches, and then Logan asked Laurel if she'd like to come with him to take Maybellene home.

While they were gone, Gemma took down a book about Chile, as well as books about Ecuador and Peru. She began reading about the long, skinny country which had it all. Mountains, seashores, deserts, icebergs. Never, in Chile, would there be a dull moment.

There was traveling for pleasure and/or adventure, as well as the sort of traveling a travel writer undertakes. There were also long stays in foreign countries by unsupervised and often naive graduate students. Was it selfish of a mother to worry about her daughter? To wish that her research could be done close to home?

The next morning, when Gemma came downstairs, Laurel was engrossed in one of the books about Ecuador. "Thanks for finding this," she said, looking up from the sofa.

"And what about Peru?" Gemma said. "I mean, Incas and all."

"Not Peru, not ever, no thank you," Laurel said. "Remember Roberto?"

"So sorry," Gemma said. "I'd forgotten he was from Peru. Did you ever hear from him?"

Laurel shook her head. "Lots of different ethnic groups in Ecuador. And absolutely gorgeous textiles. Look at this blanket! Quichua."

Gemma sat down beside her daughter.

Not far from Quito, they learned, were two tourist attractions claiming to be located on el ecuador. GPS had proven the more popular one to be close to the equator but not actually on it. The other one, identified thousands of years ago by ancient astronomers, was, according to GPS, eerily close to being correct.

Those early scientists could've belonged to either the Quitu or the Cara tribe, or perhaps both. Avid sun worshippers, they'd known that, at noon, during an equinox, there were places where the sun cast no shadow. Over the years, by marking these spots with rocks, they'd delineated the path of the Equator.

"So they were every bit as smart as Africa's ancient astronomers!" Laurel said. "Maybe even descended from them. Why couldn't Africans have sailed to South America, just as Polynesians traveled across the Pacific?"

Part VI

The Travel Writer

37

Beyond Virginia: A Magazine for Travelers
January 2017 Issue

A graduate of the University of Richmond, Gemma Sommerset divides her time between Lexington, VA, and Carmel, CA. Her previous travel articles have been published in the *Washington Post*, the *Baltimore Sun*, and the *Lynchburg News and Advance*.

Visiting Ecuador: Quito and Mindo
By Gemma Sommerset

Quito is a fascinating city, our daughter Laurel had written. Inhabited for the past 4,000 years, it was ruled by the Incas in the 1400s and then, more than a century later, almost completely destroyed and subsequently rebuilt by the Spanish conquistadores.

Laurel had been in Ecuador for more than a year when she informed her father and me, by email, that she wouldn't be writing a PhD dissertation after all and so would never become an anthropology professor.

An Ecuadorian graduate student she'd been seeing had come to the same decision about his own research in ornithology. Sami was his name, the Kichwa word for luck.

Sami's grandmother had recently died. Or, as her family would've put it, she'd "gone ahead," transitioned to the next phase of her life. Laurel and Sami were now living in her cabin, which Sami had inherited along with nearly fifty acres in the cloud forest near Mindo.

With Mindo having become a hotspot for eco-tourism, they were hoping to build six or eight new cabins and begin taking in paying guests. Was there any chance, Laurel wondered, that they could borrow some start-up money?

"In case you might be wondering," she added, "I'm pregnant."

"She's never coming back," her father said. "That Sami fellow may be good luck for her. He's bad luck for us."

"On the bright side," I said to him the next day, "I've always wanted to see the Andes."

In September of 2015, we flew to Quito, Ecuador's capital city. Laurel had encouraged us to spend a few days there, adjusting to the altitude of more than 9,000 feet. What she hadn't thought to warn us about was that thousands of Quito's citizens might be demonstrating against their President, Rafael Correa.

From our elegant suite at Swissôtel, we could see the smoke from Cotopaxi, an Andean volcano more than 19,000 feet high, which had been erupting since mid-August. In a pre-Incan language, Cotopaxi meant "neck of the moon." The eruptions meant our hopes of taking a short hike up Cotopaxi were dashed.

Nor, with human anger erupting on the streets, did it seem wise to attempt any sightseeing in Quito.

Laurel suggested that we try to get to the Intiñan Museum, the more accurate of the tourist sites marking the equator. She and Sami would then meet us there and drive us to Mindo.

Amazingly, a concierge at Swissôtel was able to find a driver willing to try to take us the sixteen miles north to the equator. Jorge received a huge tip after we'd arrived safely.

And so it was that, as we were both standing with one foot in the northern hemisphere and the other in the southern hemisphere, we saw our daughter for the first time in nearly two years. Laurel was wearing jeans and a faded denim shirt. Sami was dressed the same. Both of them were smiling.

During the two-hour drive in Sami's mud-spattered Jeep, it rained and then stopped, rained and then stopped. Mountains and clouds and mists floated by. We caught glimpses of enormous trees with gracefully waving branches. Shrubs and colorful flowers.

In Mindo, where we stopped for a late lunch, my husband lucked into finding us a hotel room.

And then Laurel and Sami took us "home," to the small cabin Sami's grandmother had left him, and the fifty acres she had grown old trying to take care of. This was where Sami envisioned a large bird sanctuary, with cabins for paying guests.

"Guests who will be helping our planet," Sami explained, "simply by staying here."

"But there is no here here." Laurel smiled. "Not yet, anyway."

Her father wanted to know who would build the cabins.

"Many willing builders," Sami said.

The sound of rushing water reminded me of hiking, years ago, in the Shenandoah National Park.

"Reminds me of Dark Hollow Falls," I said to Laurel, who then took my arm and led me down a rocky path to the Mindo River.

Mesmerized by the roiling water, I asked if there were ever canoers on the river.

"I've only seen tubers," Laurel said.

"Have you gone tubing here?"

"I've never gone tubing anywhere."

"Glad to hear it," I said to her. "And how are you feeling?"

"Everyone wants to know how I feel. I'm not sick. I'm pregnant."

"Is there a hospital in Mindo?" I asked.

"If I need a hospital, I'll go to Quito."

"You could come home, you know."

"I am home, Mother. This is my home."

We now have a granddaughter in Ecuador. Umiña (the Kichwa word for gem) has dark, serious eyes and her father's straight black hair. Long Ago Resort, near Mindo, consists of three guest cabins in the cloud forest, with plans for at least three more. There are more birds than humans, which was the plan all along.

Now that Quito has calmed down, we hope to return soon. We'll stay again at Swissôtel and dine at its excellent Japanese restaurant. We'll take a short hike up Cotopaxi before traveling on to Mindo, in Ecuador's lovely, peaceful cloud forest, where we'll stay in one of the brand-new cabins at Long Ago Resort.

Who knows? With another grandchild on the way, we may never come home.

38

Tripping
The Online Magazine for Eclectic Travelers
September 2019

Gemma Sommerset's travel writings have appeared in *Beyond Virginia*, the *Washington Post*, the *Baltimore Sun*, and the *Lynchburg News and Advance*.

A Sentimental Visit to Japan
By Gemma Sommerset

Flannery O'Connor's short story, "A Good Man is Hard to Find," has a memorable first line: "The grandmother didn't want to go to Florida." In 2018, my husband didn't want to go to Japan.

Nor, in 1945, had my father, Carson Sommerset, wanted to go anywhere near the country responsible for bombing Pearl Harbor. Having returned from fighting in Europe, he was eagerly looking forward to being discharged from the Army and returning to civilian life. I was two years old then; he and I barely knew each other.

Instead, he was soon ordered to leave for Japan, to serve in the Army of Occupation.

A good soldier obeys orders, and my father came from a long line of good soldiers, dating back to the Civil War, and probably even before that. So, in the fall of 1945, having boarded a ship in San Francisco, and after enduring week after week of extreme seasickness, Captain Carson Sommerset disembarked in Tokyo. From there, he was moved around from one town to another, as if the Army weren't quite sure what, exactly, they were supposed to be doing in Japan.

During his six months there, he wrote wonderful letters home to my mother. I knew they existed but, for whatever reason, didn't read the letters until both of my parents had passed away.

My father's letters paint an intriguing picture of the country he'd disliked, at first, but gradually came to admire.

Hoping the letters might provide an itinerary for us, I asked my husband to read them. Despite enjoying the engaging descriptions and wry humor, he very sensibly suggested that the various airport hangars and other makeshift troop quarters where my father had been stationed would surely have been torn down by now. He was also (unreasonably, I thought) worried about continuing radiation from the 2011 Fukushima power plant disaster.

So we compromised. A few days in Tokyo. Perhaps a short hike up Mount Fuji, which my father had admired wistfully from a distance. And a stay in the place where my father had been happiest, the Fujiya Hotel in Miyanoshita, founded in 1878 and, amazingly, still open, with excellent reviews on its website. Also amazing was the fact that I was able to make a reservation for three nights in the Carnation room, where my father had stayed when he was there.

Here's how he'd described the hotel in a letter to my mother:

Nov. 8, 1945
Miyanoshita

Dearest Maryl,

Your undeserving husband has just fallen into a mighty soft deal. Tuesday morning, I was minding my S-2 business in the office when the Colonel came banging in (of course I had him go back and knock) and asked if I wanted to go to a resort hotel for 6 days temporary duty (doesn't count against my leave). He also planned to send Col. W. I told him I had no need for rest or recuperation but of course would be tickled to go. About two, I was in Kofu at the Military Gov't office transacting some business when the Adjutant called and said I had to catch a 3:30 train. I tore out to camp, threw some things in my Valetpak and took off again for the station, receiving my orders on the fly. We (the Regt.) have a special car on the train to Tokyo and that was fine, but it was late and I had to find out from the Japanese how to get across Tokyo to the station from which I was to catch a train. Finally made it. Finally caught a train to Odawara on the coast below here but didn't get there till almost eleven and the last electric train left for the hotel at eight, which of course no one had told me. I scared the station-master half to death but couldn't phone here for a jeep. ("The line it is damage.") So I found an MP post in the police station, borrowed a blanket and a cot and nearly froze all the rest of the night. Caught the 6:30 tram up the mountain — it (the tram) had to have the balance and agility of a mountain goat -- and got to Miyanoshita not long after seven. Walked, still with Valetpak, about 300 yards to the hotel, and it was all worth it. I'm in Carnation, a very fine room in the new wing assigned to the officers of the Allied Powers. Was in Spirea until Major Shields came last night by jeep, replacing Col. W. who couldn't come. He's in with me. All the rooms are named for flowers, and we're right over some hot springs. There's a "Dream Pool," "Mermaid's Pool," "Roman Aquarium," and "Bath of Eternal Youth," to the last of which I shall soon repair to wash off the day's grime. White Sulphur Springs is the only thing I've seen to compare with this place. In this wing (the Flower Palace) the rooms are all modern and each decorated differently. The older part of the hotel is occupied by civilians: Germans, Swedes, Swiss, Siamese, and Turkish, as well as some Japs -- men, women, and children. Grand Hotel. Sure wish you were here, Honey. Our east window looks down a very steep valley with the town hanging on the shoulder. This morning, it being very clear, we could see the ocean (Sagami Bay). On the south we're almost against the face of a very steep and high bluff all beforested with evergreens, some laurel, and others, which are now turning red, orange, and yellow. The food is good, the service is excellent, and isn't the Army a terrible life?

I'm actually going walking tomorrow, out to the point of a ridge looking down toward the bay. Slept three hours yesterday afternoon and nine last night, am clean and feeling wonderful. Sure wish you were here.

Will write again before I leave. Keep sweet, tell Daughter to be good, and keep writing. The only reason I didn't want to come down here was I wouldn't have any mail for six days.
'Bye.

All my love,
Carson

At more than 12,000 feet high, Mount Fuji is visible from nearly anywhere in Japan. My husband and

I quickly agreed that we shouldn't try to climb to the top. We're too old to spend the night in a hut on the way up and/or back down. Instead, we hired a driver, in nearby Kofu, to take us as close as we could get by car.

I'd noticed, on a map, an area called the Sea of Trees, on Mount Fuji's northwestern slopes. Intrigued, I asked our tall, slender driver if he could take us there.

Ren had spent two years at UCLA. "Absolutely not," he replied. "No way."

"Why not?" my husband said. "We love forests. The bigger the better."

"That one's too big. People get lost. All the time."

"But surely there's a path," I said. "We'll stay on the main path, then simply turn around and follow it back. We won't stay long, I promise."

"Not so simple," Ren said. "Very old virgin forest, dating back to when Fuji erupted in the year 864. Primeval. The leaves are always green, so it's dark all year long. People go in, but with no sunlight, they can't find their way back out. I'm telling you this for your own good."

"Then tell us more," my husband said. "Tell us what you're not saying."

Slowly, reluctantly, Ren tried to explain. The trees had odd shapes and strange roots, like scary monsters.

There were ghosts in the forest—yūrei . Some people, after having left the paved path, would attach ribbons to the trees so as to be able to find their way back. Or, if they decided to go through with it, so that their loved ones would be able to find their dead bodies. In olden times, families would abandon their grandparents, leave them deep in the dark forest to die.

"The Sea of Trees is haunted," I said when he'd finished.

"Big time," Ren said. "Dark forest, dark stories, dark history. I will not take you there."

"All right, then," my husband said. "Is there an easy trail where the three of us could take a short hike up Mount Fuji?"

"Of course," Ren said.

And so we can honestly claim to have hiked up Mount Fuji. We just don't say how far up.

Although we did try, our dream of forest bathing, or shinrin-yoku, in the country where the term originated, never came true. It's possible we'd simply chosen the wrong forest. How can one truly *bathe* when, with hundreds of others on the same path, there's a total lack of either solitude or privacy?

However, one afternoon, near Tokyo, we happened

upon a bamboo forest made up of thousands and thousands of nearly identical, very tall, green stalks. Multilingual signs and sturdy railings prevented anyone from leaving the paved pathway.

For a while, at least, we were miraculously alone on the path. Above us, in the canopy, a sudden wind was playing the bamboo like an instrument—rustling the leaves and causing the trunks to bend and creak and tap against each other.

"We're forest bathing to music," I whispered.

"A heavenly choir," my husband said, taking my hand.

"Except that this isn't really a forest. Bamboo is a kind of grass, not a tree."

"Shhh," he said. "Listen up."

Late one night, during our stay in the Carnation Room at the Fujiya Hotel, I was awakened by groans.

"A nightmare," my husband said. "With hundreds of ribbons. Maybe thousands. Iridescent ribbons."

"In the Sea of Trees?" I asked.

"The ribbons were everywhere. They were strangling people."

"It was just a dream." I touched his cheek. "You're feverish."

"But why even bother with ribbons? Either you want to die, or you don't. And if you do, then go ahead, but don't make your loved ones have to come find you in a scary forest. That's chicken-shit. Just shoot yourself in the living room. Or the kitchen, where it'll be easier to clean up."

I took his hand. It was cold as ice.

"Your father stayed in this room?" he said after a while.

"Yes," I said. "I keep imagining he's still here."

"I didn't have a father."

"I know."

"I know you think you know," he said. "But you don't really."

Japan came home with us. That happens sometimes. You go somewhere, you have a wonderful time, but when it's over, the trip haunts you. It won't let go.

One morning, nearly a year after we'd returned to California, I found a note on our kitchen table. *In to the wodes I go. No ribones.*

My first thought was: what has happened to his spelling?

Then it hit me, and I panicked.

Where was he not taking ribbons? Which woods?

Our car was gone. I alerted the park authorities in Big Sur and gave them our phone number, our license plate number, and a description of our car. Buzzard's Roost, I told them, was my husband's favorite spot. I then borrowed a neighbor's car and hurried down to Big Sur myself.

Having hiked up to Buzzards Roost, I called out for him, frantically.

I wasn't really expecting an answer. I knew he didn't want to be found.

No ribbons.

It was a few days before I was able to reach our younger daughter, who lives in Ecuador. By then, our older daughter had flown in from Virginia, where, except for road trips to Kentucky to visit her in-laws, and a summer job in DC, she has spent her entire life.

She tells me not to blame myself.

Assures me that if it was Alzheimer's setting in, then he had done me a favor. Reminds me how lucky I was to have visited Japan with him.

I don't mention the Sea of Trees. Don't say anything about the ribbons Ren told us about.

I don't tell anyone.

39

To Whom It May Concern:
Please fill in the blanks and send to the *Lexington News-Gazette*.

Gemma Sommerset, age ___, of Lexington, VA, began her next journey on ________ (month, day, year). That morning, as usual, she'd greeted the sunrise from her beloved deck. Having finished her thermos of coffee, she started down the steps. That's when decades of dire predictions came true. After tumbling head over heels, she lay unconscious in the grass for hours. It was nearly dusk when she was finally rescued. The deer, a doe, knew exactly what to do. As did Gemma. Soon, without a saddle or reins to hang onto, she was soaring over her neighbors' fences, then flying downhill through the woods. By the time they reached Woods Creek, night had fallen. Gemma dismounted and smiled at the small crowd who'd assembled to greet her. Her brother, her parents, and

both of her husbands smiled back.
 "Come with us," they whispered.
 And she did.

About the Author

A former librarian at Johns Hopkins University, Jill Coupe has an MFA in fiction from Warren Wilson College. Having grown up in Knoxville, Tennessee, she (like Gemma) has always loved the Southern Appalachians. She won the 2017 IPPY Gold Medal for Regional Fiction South for her novel *True Stories at the Smoky View* (She Writes Press, 2016) and the 2021 IPPY Silver Medal for Multicultural Fiction for *Beginning with Cannonballs* (She Writes Press, 2020). Jill currently lives in Southern Vermont. Visit her website, jillmcoupe.com, to learn more.

We Grow Our Books in Montpelier, Vermont

Learn more about our titles in Fiction, Non-fiction, Poetry and Children's Literature at the QR code below or visit www.rootstockpublishing.com.